C000254865

Siân James was brought █████████████████
Her first novel, *One Af*█████████████████
First Novel Award; he██████████████████████
Yorkshire Post Best Nove████████, her fifth, *Dragons and Roses* won a Welsh Arts Council prize and a collection of short stories, *Not Singing, Exactly*, won the Welsh Arts Council Book of the Year Award.

Summer Storm is her tenth published novel and the third published by Piatkus, *Love & War* and *Two Loves* being the others. She has four grown-up children and one grandchild, and now lives in Warwickshire.

Also by Siân James

Love & War
Two Loves

Summer
Storm

Siân James

PIATKUS

First published in Great Britain in 1998 by
Judy Piatkus (Publishers) Ltd of
5 Windmill Street, London W1P 1HF

This edition published 1999

A catalogue record for this book is available from the British LIbrary.

ISBN 0 7499 3108 6

Set in Times by
Wyvern 21 Ltd, Bristol

Printed and bound in Great Britain by
Mackays of Chatham plc, Chatham, Kent

For my family with love

Chapter 1

The Radio Three concert – Elgar and Vaughan Williams – comes to an end. I close the library book I'm trying to read and lay it aside.

It's a sultry evening, the sky plum-coloured, a threat of thunder in the air.

Peter has been standing at the window for almost an hour, still as a shadow.

'Peter,' I hear myself say, 'you really must pull yourself together.'

The dense, after-music silence of the room is suddenly full of echoes; pullyourselftogether, pullyourselftogether, pullyourselftogether; a hundred echoes.

He turns towards me and our eyes meet. Why do I go on? It's hopeless.

To me, the surprise is that his affair with Alice lasted as long as it did.

He's not her type: he's quiet and stolid; he wears sports jackets and trousers with creases; his pale-brown eyes are clear and innocent. (Once or twice, though, when Alice said or did something particularly outrageous, I noticed a spark of anger in them, but then a lizard-blink and emptiness again.)

My daughter, Alice, left here quite suddenly about three weeks ago, and neither of us has heard from her since.

I suppose she had a perfect right to go. She's recently left college and managed to get a good, or at least a well-paid, job, starting next month. She even has some money out of a small legacy my great-aunt left her last year. And after all, Peter doesn't own her; by this time I'm not even sure whether he has any shares in her.

'Peter,' I say, for the fortieth or fiftieth time, 'isn't it natural that she should want a holiday? She's been working hard, she needs change, she needs stimulation. If she didn't tell you she was going to be away so long, well, I'm sorry. She can be thoughtless. But you know that already. You know already how impulsive she is.'

I'm sure Alice took it for granted that he'd move back to his flat as soon as she left. But no, he seems to need to be here, so that I, at least, may be aware of all he's going through.

'Oh Peter, I know it's rotten for you, but I've tried to help you as much as I can . . . Well, I've advised you to get back to your flat, for a start. I honestly think it would be much better for you to be with your friends than to be stuck here with me.'

It would be much better for me, too, but I'm doing my best not to think of that.

'They're not your friends? All right, your colleagues, your flatmates. It would surely be better for you to have something to do in the evenings, instead of just sitting around, listening for the telephone.'

He gazes intently at me, as though I'm saying all this for the first time.

'You'd certainly have to do some shopping and some cooking, wouldn't you? Don't you all take it in turn to get the evening meal? Even that would take your mind off Alice for an hour or so. And afterwards you could go out for a drink with someone. There must be one of them you could talk to. What about Clementine? You said she was nice.'

'Clementine,' he says, nodding his head gravely. And after several seconds, 'Oh yes. Clementine.'

'People have to get over things, Peter. I mean, if it is over between you and Alice, you'll just have to accept it. Couldn't you try to persuade yourself that it might be all for the best? If you're not right for each other, isn't it better to find out sooner rather than later?'

He could never accept that. Now or later.

'You don't think you could try to get a week off work to go home to your parents? You haven't been home all this year. Being with different people in a different place might give you some different ideas. You might decide to ring up some of your old friends. To see how they're making out ... Oh Peter, you must have had some girlfriends before Alice. You can't try to tell me that a man of twenty-five has no past.'

He doesn't think he could go home. Or back to the flat. He says Alice promised to phone him here, in this house.

Oh God, he's going to stay here for ever.

To think how pleased I was when she first brought him home, so clean-cut and wholesome; so different from her usual entourage. I thought it was a sign that she was growing up.

Even the fact that he was a vicar's son and one of five children was surprisingly comforting.

'He works with computers,' she'd said, and I'd hastily revised my previous opinion that children at school who forged ahead with computer study were brain-clever but soul-retarded.

Her previous boyfriends had been of quite another type; bright, brash, extrovert, predatory. Peter was polite and reserved. She seemed to regard him with a mixture of pride and disbelief. She looked at him like a nanny looking at a very well-behaved child, never like a young woman looking at her lover.

'I bet you a quid, he's the sort who'll sink to his knees and propose to me,' she said one evening a few weeks ago, 'and I won't know whether to cry or die laughing.'

'There are still people who believe in marriage,' I said, 'even if you don't.'

She turned to me. 'Sometimes I do believe in it. And if I was the marrying kind, Peter would definitely be high on my list.

3

He's so considerate. Have you noticed how he leaves the bath? How he tidies my room? He has no bad habits: he doesn't read or think; he doesn't talk about Life all the time. Think what a restful time I could have with him.'

'But you don't love him.'

'He doesn't excite me. Is that what you mean?'

'I suppose it is.'

'Did David excite you?'

'Oh yes. All the time.'

But I mustn't think of David.

Alice was at art college in Brighton until she graduated this year with an upper second. While she was away, it probably gave her some pleasure to think of Peter back here waiting for her. She probably even enjoyed having him visit her from time to time.

It was when she got back here in the middle of June and he practically moved in with us that it became too much for her.

She rang me at school one lunchtime. 'Hi Mum,' she said. 'I'm ringing to say goodbye. I'll be gone by the time you get back. Look after yourself. Don't work too hard and don't forget the vitamin pills.'

'OK love,' I said. 'Have a good time. Take care.'

I didn't ask where she was going. I assumed she was off to London or to Brighton for a few days. I also assumed that Peter would be going with her.

When I got back after a long and weary end-of-term Wednesday, I was thinking of a quiet evening, of a beer and a sandwich on the patio and an early night.

An early night? A quiet beginning to a well-earned holiday? Forget it.

'Why didn't you ask her where she was going? Didn't you worry when she rang you out of the blue and said she was off? Didn't you think it was odd? How did she sound? Did she sound angry? Did she sound miserable?

The questions have been going on ever since . . .

And when he's not petulant, he's pathetic.

'I love her,' he says. 'Don't ask me to forget her.'

So quietly and simply he says it, that it gets to me again. 'But you must try,' I say. 'Look around you at any crowd of people,' I say, 'and I'm sure about half of them have someone they can't forget. All right, you can't forget Alice. But life goes on.'

We look deeply at each other. Is it possible that I'm getting through to him? Would it help if I told him about David? About how things are with me?

No. His mood has swung round again. 'Did she tell you how long she was going to be away? Didn't she say why she was going? Didn't you ask her why? Why didn't you?'

Oh Peter, I don't feel I can take much more.

I decide to phone my friend Dilys. Up to now, I've tried to tell myself that I can manage this without her, but I suddenly realise I can't.

Dilys has three sons, two ex-husbands and a vast experience, she says, of men's perversity.

Leave him to me, she says; she has the knack, she says, of getting rid of people gracefully.

Her boys, or at least the older two, Gareth and Tom, have gone through every possible difficult stage, but by this time, they're at least being difficult away from home. Gareth is at Durham University reading French – at the moment he's directing a play by a Ghanaian writer at the Edinburgh Fringe – while Tom, reading English at Bristol, has just got together his first collection of poetry, currently being turned down, according to Dilys, by all the very best publishers. At the moment he's in Turkey with his father.

'All right,' she says, 'if you don't want me to throw him out' (I have memories of her flinging open her front door and shouting, C'mon you lot, time to go) 'I'll come round and take him off your hands for an hour or two. That's the least I can do. And I'll get Hywel to come with me, to do your lawn.'

Hywel, thirteen, is the son of her second marriage; a large, placid, uncomplicated boy who plays rugby and cricket and tells Irishman jokes.

Five minutes later she appears, wearing a slinky black dress and silver eye-shadow. Her dark hair is short and curly, her skin brown and smooth. She's exactly the same age as I am – forty-two – but she often looks twenty-nine, while I often look forty-two.

'The best think you can do,' she says at the door, 'is to go away to Greece. If he wants to stay on in the house, then let him. It might save you a burglary.'

But I can't afford to go to Greece or anywhere else. The new Metro was instead of a holiday. I remind her of this.

'Oh nonsense. How can you pretend to be poor with a B allowance teacher's salary. If you're poor, what am I? I haven't had work for thirty-two weeks, not even an advert.'

When I first knew Dilys, she was far too high-minded to do adverts, even voice-overs. At the beginning of her career, she worked in experimental theatre. Two marriages and three children later, she does Sunshine Shampoo, Let Nature's gold glisten in your hair, Slimkwik Meals, Gourmet satisfaction in a tea-cup, and the occasional small part in 'God's World' on Channel Four.

She doesn't like me to remind her that she turned down her Big Break – a leading part with a leading theatre company – because she felt she couldn't leave the boys. Hywel was only three then, and Gareth – ten – was going through a particularly difficult stage. Well, he usually was, but this was shoplifting, to which second husband, Ralph, was dourly over-reacting.

We go into the sitting-room where Peter is now sitting hunched-up and switched-off in front of the switched-off television.

'Listen,' Dilys says, tapping him on the shoulder with her tiny thirties handbag, 'how about that drink we talked about last week?'

Her voice is ever soft, gentle and low, an excellent thing in advertising.

Peter gets to his feet, adjusting his tie and looking startled.

6

'Gosh, I'm sorry,' Dilys says, her eyelashes fluttering like startled bees, 'I suppose I shouldn't have mentioned it in front of Sarah.'

'Don't be silly,' I say. 'I'd trust you with my own grandfather. Off you go, Peter. It'll do you good.'

I know perfectly well that a trip to the local pub won't do him any good at all. A world tour, that nineteenth-century cure for a broken heart, wouldn't do Peter any good. He'd be too self-absorbed to notice the pyramids. He'd go on talking about Alice, how she'd promised him this, that and the other, for the whole length of the Great Wall.

However, knowing that someone else is coping with him does me a power of good. I luxuriate in an hour alone, yawning in front of the television and thinking about Dilys, about what a good friend she is.

By this time, I can hardly imagine life without her; she's stood by me through so much. She never cared for David, could never understand what he meant to me, but when I got that letter from him last year, she stayed with me day and night for almost a week, letting me talk and cry, getting me to eat and look after myself.

These days, I don't let myself think about David. The fact is that I've got used to being without him. When I wake up, it's not to a gripping pain, new every morning, but to yesterday's dull acceptance, a deadness. I don't let myself think about David.

When Dilys and Peter return from the pub, they're both looking morose.

'Go and make us some coffee, love,' she tells him, 'and if you can cut bread, I'd like some thin bread and butter with it.'

Her voice is smooth, but I detect a layer of ice on the 'if you can cut bread' and I look at her expectantly, my arms pulled tight across my stomach. Dilys will have got something sorted out, I know.

'Listen,' she says, as soon as he's out of the room, 'I've managed to drag something out of him. Alice is pregnant. Now, stop looking like that. It can happen to anyone. The reason I'm telling you is this: he wanted them to get married and had even started making the arrangements. So it's pretty obvious that she couldn't face it, and decided on an abortion, followed by a holiday to get over it. And she'll probably be home any day now and I think it's essential that you've thrown him out of here before she comes. She's got a right to expect that of you.'

'Why hasn't she phoned me?' I ask. I shake my head, trying to get rid of a sizzling noise in my ears.

I'd counted on her being happy, having an adventure somewhere, kicking up her heels.

'Why hasn't she phoned me?' I ask again.

'She's afraid that lout might answer the phone, that's why.'

'So why hasn't she phoned me during the day when he's at work? And he's not a lout.' (Though exasperating, God knows.)

He comes in with the coffee, carrying the tray stiffly in front of him as though it's a religious offering.

'Look at him,' Dilys says. 'Six foot two in his stockinged feet and every inch a man. What a chest. What muscles. When you went into computers, Peter, the country lost a wonderful navvy. Didn't you ever think of a career on the stage? Sarah, wouldn't he make a wonderful Mark Anthony? Stripped for the Games? Wouldn't he make a wonderful scene-shifter? Look at him with that coffee-table. Look at this bread-and-butter. You wouldn't get better than this at the Ritz.'

I can't smile, because there are still little tremors of fear in my stomach.

We drink coffee and Dilys puts on some music.

'I think I'll go to bed,' I say, my voice sounding as it does when I'm losing an argument with 5C.

I drag myself out of my chair and go to bed.

I don't manage to sleep. She's twenty-two, I'm telling myself one minute, and she's been looking after herself for years. If she's pregnant, she should have told me about it, I'm telling myself the next.

8

When I found out I was pregnant, I was in a state of terror, even though I had a house and a husband. I mean, a husband and a house. The fact is that I'd hardly had time to get used to having a husband, while I've still got the house. My husband was drowned – in front of my eyes, I usually say at this point, though in fact he was much too far out for me to have seen anything – when we'd only been married four months.

I got married at nineteen to the first man who asked me, because I couldn't think of anything better to do. Alice is far more mature and sophisticated than I was. She had a normal upbringing with plenty of friends of both sexes. She's had choices, which is more than I did. She's got a good mind, a wise head on her shoulders, and if she's decided to have an abortion, it's the right thing for her.

But why didn't she tell me about it? Why?

My pillow is wet.

Some time later, there's a tiny knock at my bedroom door and Dilys comes in.

'OK,' she says, 'I've got it sorted out. It's difficult to get through to Peter, but when you do, boy, he reverberates with understanding. He's moving back to his flat first thing in the morning.'

I look at her doubtfully and blow my nose.

'There was talk in the Avenue, I said, about you having a man in the house, and you could lose your job if it went any further.'

'Oh, Dilys.'

'I was surprised, I said, that he hadn't considered the implications himself, he being a man of the world. He said I had old-fashioned values and he honoured me for them. Then he said something pretty about his mother.'

'I can't understand why she didn't tell me she was pregnant,' I said.

'I'll tell you why, stupid. She was afraid you'd try to persuade her to have the baby, that's why. Mothers always do. Why do you think I had Gareth?'

'Why hasn't she phoned me? She's been gone almost a month. She usually phones once a week, at the very least. Do you think she's all right?'

'Of course she's all right. She's on a beach somewhere. I can see her now. Having a wonderful time.'

'At this time of night?'

'A moonlight party. A barbecue on the white sands. Tequila. Lovely seafood . . . Oh, I'd better not say any more or you'll be worrying about food poisoning. Listen, Sarah, Alice is fine. She'll always be fine because she's tough and resilient. You're the one I worry about. You've had a very hard year, and now you say you're not going on holiday.'

I have had a hard year, an awful year. But I'm not going to think about it tonight.

'Anyway, Sarah, he's coming home with me now. I'll just give him a drink to cheer him up. You've got nothing but sherry.'

'He's had all my whisky and I'm not getting him any more. It makes him worse.'

'Quite right. I'll see you in the morning, then.'

'Good-night, Dilys. Thanks for coming over. Thanks for everything.'

Chapter 2

'The only thing I don't understand is why you told me Hywel was coming with you. To do my lawn.'

'Oh Sarah, that means you don't believe me.'

'I do believe you, Dilys. Honestly. Please don't cry again, love. Please. I believe you. I believe you. Ten thousand times, I believe you. You were raped. I believe you.'

'Then why pick on that one thing I know sounds suspicious. That bloody inspector's gone on and on about it. Can you please believe that I'd forgotten that Hywel was away when you phoned – he only went at teatime yesterday – and having said that he would be coming to do your lawn, I didn't like to correct myself. I'll tell you why. Because I hate it when you think I'm a terrible mother. How could she forget where her little darling is, you'd be thinking, and him only twelve.'

'Thirteen.'

'Thirteen, then.'

'But I wouldn't have thought that. I think you're a marvellous mother. It does children good to be forgotten occasionally. Neglect is what they thrive on; loving neglect. Some famous child psychologist said that.'

'A marvellous mother! They think I'm a vindictive nymphomaniac. Oh, Sarah, do you think I was wrong to call the police? Do you think I've made too much fuss about it? Tell me honestly.'

'Of course I don't. How could I think you're making too much fuss about it? It's sickening. I can hardly bear to think about it. I've never had that much time for Peter, but now . . . well, I just hate him. Why are they searching his room?'

'Perhaps they think he's that Suffolk rapist they've been looking for.'

'Perhaps he is.'

I try to smile.

We're in Dilys's sitting-room. She's still in her green cotton dressing-gown; her feet are bare. (Pretty feet, bony and brown, toenails painted blotting-paper pink.)

She looks much the same as usual, except that there are two spots of colour on her cheekbones. Somehow, I expected her to look entirely different: older and more placid, like someone just out of anaesthetic.

It's the sitting-room that seems to have changed. I usually envy Dilys her flair for interior design: the startling colours she chooses, the way she manages to create such exotic effects with second-hand furniture, shabby Persian rugs – which would be worth a fortune, she says, if they weren't threadbare – and piles of silk cushions made from Liberty remnants.

Today, it all seems tawdry and slightly pathetic.

I don't feel I can bear the glassy tinkle of that fall of wind bells over the French doors for much longer.

'Do you want to shut the window?' Dilys asks, following my glance. 'Shall we have the heating on? Isn't it cold suddenly?'

For the first time, I notice how tense she is, her fists clenched and white at the knuckles.

'Shall I put some music on?' I ask.

She doesn't answer. The air tightens around us. We can't seem to break the silence. We both sigh.

'You see, they can't believe I really minded it,' she says at last. 'I suppose they think any woman who's been married twice should be used to all sorts of rough treatment. I mean, that's the world they know. And then, of course, they asked me how many other men I'd slept with.'

12

'They had no right to ask you that. They're not supposed to make moral judgements.'

'I told them anyway. Two marriages, two long-term relationships and one short.'

'You shouldn't have told them any of that. It's nothing to do with them. It won't help you.'

'Why? Do you think it's excessive? For twenty-odd years?'

'No, but they will. Two long-term affairs and one short. They'll think it's really sordid.'

'Will they?'

'No, I'm sure they won't. I'm just over-anxious.'

'Peter was still here when they came. He was slumped in that chair, looking like a zombie, until the moment he heard them arrive, then he sat up and managed to look quite composed. Oh God, how many rapists look as thoroughly normal and decent as that great booby? Wouldn't you believe he was innocent? If you didn't know me? You can understand them doubting my version of it, can't you?'

She didn't wait for my answer.

'He told them I'd been perfectly willing all along. Indeed, he intimated – though not in actual words, which wouldn't be gentle-manly – that I'd made the first moves; said I'd invited him here as soon as you'd gone to bed; things like that. And then he took great pains to explain that he was engaged to your daughter, inferring that I was cooking up this rape charge because I was ashamed of betraying your trust. That's why I had to bring you into it – you do understand, don't you? At least you could confirm that you'd asked me over to take him off your hands for a while.'

'Yes of course. Listen, I'm sure they're not really taken in by him.'

(In fact, I'm not at all sure. That inspector who interviewed me seemed firmly on Peter's side. Or was that a way of making me lose my temper and reveal things I didn't intend to?)

Dilys starts to cry, hard tearing sobs that make her sound very young and frightened.

I go over and sit by her side, unable to think of anything

to say or do. I'm so anxious about her that I can't swallow properly; there's a lump in my throat which seems large as an egg.

'Were you crying when they were here?' I ask, when she's almost recovered; fetching up trembling breaths from the pit of her stomach.

'Of course I was crying. I'd been hurt and frightened. You've no idea what it's like, Sarah, you can't have. When someone suddenly becomes someone else, someone inhuman, some great 'thing'. He was pressing me down by my elbows so that I couldn't move, and however much I tried to struggle I couldn't stop him. Oh, it was so humiliating and horrible. Of course I was crying.'

'They'll believe you,' I say.

'Will they? When Peter kept telling them about my being a professional actress? They kept saying he wasn't to interrupt me, but they seemed terribly interested every time he did.'

'Don't go on. It upsets you too much.'

'It was the woman – the constable – who was doing all the questioning. The inspector was just listening and filing away all my answers in his thick skull. But he was the more unsympathetic. Didn't you think he was unsympathetic?'

'Perhaps it was just his manner. I suppose he was only trying to get at the truth.'

'And then the woman asked whether I'd be willing to have a medical examination. I said I would, but she wouldn't let me phone Dr Francis. I had to go with them to the bloody police station. She said their doctor would be more thorough, would know exactly what to look for and so on. And then the inspector told Peter he had to go to the Police Station as well. I don't think they asked his consent. Oh, I can't remember. Anyway they took us in two different cars. I didn't see him afterwards. Oh God, I hope I'll never see him again. Only I'll have to in court. Unless they throw the case out.'

'They won't. They'll believe you. Of course they will.'

'If only I'd been able to tear his face. God, how I wanted to.

14

If only I'd been able to knee him in the groin or kick his skins. There'd have been something to show. I couldn't move. He was so strong, I couldn't move. There'll be nothing to show.'

'They'll see something.'

'Nothing.'

She's pressing her mouth with the knuckle of her right hand, trying to keep it from trembling. 'Nothing. They won't want to see anything. The police doctor seemed so tired and cynical. I'm quite sure he didn't believe me. I was kept waiting for hours – it seemed like hours – in this horrible bleak, cold room. Oh, they'll throw the case out, I'm sure. They'll think I led him on. The big innocent, so young and clean-looking. The inspector kept on about the difference in our ages. "How old is your eldest son?" he asked. "Nearly twenty-one." "I see. Just three years younger than the accused." "That's right." "And you are? Forty-three next birthday?" "That's right. Still the same as when you asked me last." God, I hate policemen.'

'By the way, I phoned Ralph and asked him to come over.'

'You what?'

She sits up angrily. It's the best thing I could have done. She's furious, now, instead of pathetic. 'Ralph?'

'Well, he's a police officer, too. He'll give you . . . you know . . . respectability.'

'Respectability? I don't want any bloody thing from Ralph. Respectability? Stuff him.'

'And don't say things like that. Please. He was very sympathetic.'

'No, he wasn't. He might be concerned. In case Hywel gets dragged into it. But he doesn't know how to be sympathetic towards me. Serves you bloody well right, he'll say. Why couldn't you wear a pebble-dash two-piece like my mother used to.'

'Pebble-dash is what they put on houses.'

'Yes. That's what he'd have liked me to go around in. Like that bloody inspector. "Wasn't that rather a provocative dress to be wearing at that time of night?" As though you can only wear sexy dresses to charity coffee mornings. Oh, Sarah, everybody gets me wrong.'

'Don't be silly. You like looking attractive, and more attractive than anyone else. What's wrong with that? You like people to notice you. That's what you were trained for, what's wrong with that?'

'Stuff Ralph. I wish you hadn't asked him to come. It shows you think I'm in a very weak position.'

'It doesn't. It shows I want you to be in a very strong position. Look, I'll stay with you the whole time he's here if you like.'

'Bloody Ralph! I bet he'll be expecting me to have a meal waiting for him, too.'

'No, he won't. Come on, he's not as bad as you make out.'

'Yes he is. He's worse. Ralph was my biggest mistake. What made me fall for such a depressing-looking man with absolutely no sense of humour? I thought he was going to save me in some way, I suppose, teach me to grow up or something. All he did was moan and complain and I didn't change at all.'

'He's still very fond of you.'

'Big deal! Well, now I don't even want to change. I may be lightweight but at least I'm not dull or pompous.'

Her voice trails off and she yawns. She's far more herself by this time. I can breathe fairly easily again, let the tension flow from my shoulders.

'That big oaf couldn't possibly have thought I was leading him on. I was horrible to him. I had one thing on my mind and that was to bring him down to earth as far as Alice was concerned. She's not going to marry you, I kept saying. Don't kid yourself. Even if she's pregnant she's not going to marry you. She likes her freedom too much. She's a high flier, that one. She's not for you, Sonny. I suppose I maddened him. Rape isn't to do with sex. He didn't want to have sex with me, he wanted to kill me. And for a while I thought he was going to. But then, quite suddenly, the fit left him.'

16

'Did he have too much to drink?' (I'm trying to calm her again.)

'Too much to drink? No, he didn't. Don't make excuses for him, Sarah. He had a beer in the pub. Two beers. No, a pint and then a half. That's all. We only had coffee in your house. And then I gave him a whisky here. That's all. And after a bit, I said I wanted to go to bed. I stood up and he came towards me – to kiss me good-night as I thought. And suddenly – it was just here – he got hold of me round the arms and pushed me back on to the sofa.'

'Oh God.'

'He was like an animal. I tried to hit him, I tried to scratch him, but he was too strong. God, he's twice my size.'

'Why don't you have a drop of brandy?'

I'm not sure that she ought to have a drink after the sedatives, but she's started to shiver again, so I get up and pour her a very small one. We sit for a time without speaking.

Then Ralph comes to the door and I let him in.

I can't help liking Ralph, though I feel some disloyalty in admitting it nowadays.

He's a large, solid man who takes himself very seriously. He seldom smiles, and looks rather embarrassed when he does, as though he's belched or done something to be ashamed of. His large face, rubbery and impassive, is so like a comedian's that I was never quite able to accept that he actually meant the outrageously chauvinistic things he used to come out with.

When he and Dilys moved into No. 8, they had only recently got married and Hywel was born the next year. Ralph was already forty then, and his pride in the baby and his efforts to conceal it was another thing I found endearing. 'Come, come, Sarah, you can't actually say that a six-week-old baby has any pretentions to beauty.' 'You really think he's advanced for his age? This little mutt?'

When Dilys told me they were splitting up, I could hardly believe it. I always half believed that their frequent quarrels were put on to entertain me. For a long time I expected them to get together again in the best domestic-comedy tradition.

It wasn't until he announced his intention of getting married again, to a large, attractive policewoman – Liz – that I gave up trying to mend the breach between them.

('Liz is exactly right for him,' Dilys said when she first met her. 'She's very calm and steadfast with a high forehead like Prince Albert. Yes, it's Prince Albert she reminds me of.' By this time she likes her, though, because Hywel does.)

'I don't know what I can do,' Ralph says quietly while we're still in the hall. 'I've come, but I don't know what good I can do.'

'Anyway, thanks,' I say, taking him in to the sitting-room.

'Christ, she looks terrible,' he says.

He drags a chair closer to the sofa where Dilys is lying and sits down facing her. 'How do you feel, love?'

'I suppose you're used to this sort of scene,' Dilys says coldly. 'I suppose you'd be as beastly as the bloody inspector who's been here half the morning.'

He shrugs his shoulders. 'It's not exactly an easy job,' he says. 'These days we send a woman to our rape victims. They're supposed to be more sympathetic.'

'The policewoman who came here didn't seem all that sympathetic. She asked my age about half a dozen times. ''Forty-three next birthday,'' she kept repeating after me, as though I should know better than to be raped at that advanced age. If only I was a grandmother. Everyone drools over grandmothers. Is it my fault that Gareth and Tom are too clever to settle down?'

'Where's Hywel?' Ralph asks.

'He's at Richard's. At the farm. He'll be home about seven. He's got badminton tonight.'

'Would you like me to have him for a while? Take him off your hands for a few days? I'm sure Liz wouldn't mind. I don't suppose you want to tell him about all this?'

'I'm certainly not going out of my way to try to keep it from him. As though I'm ashamed of it. Knowing about it might do him some good.'

'All the same, it might be better if his father were to tell him,' I say.

(What I really want is for Ralph to stay. Looking every inch a police inspector, his presence can't fail but help Dilys.)

'What about some egg and chips?' I ask him.

'Fancy remembering my favourite meal,' he says, smiling a little for the first time.

'Don't forget the ketchup and the Daddies sauce,' Dilys says, her eyes sharp as lances.

There are frozen chips in the freezer so I very quickly rustle up a meal; two gooey eggs, chips and peas, bread-and-butter and a pot of tea, and take it in on a tray.

As I kick open the door, I see that Ralph is holding one of Dilys's hands. She's looking a little less tense, he probably as relaxed as any police officer can look when not actually making an arrest.

'I'll go back home for a while,' I say. 'In case Alice is trying to ring me. I've got a feeling she'll ring me today.'

'Sarah, don't worry about Alice,' Dilys says. 'Alice knows how to look after herself, I promise you.'

'You'll come back later, won't you?' Ralph asks me. 'I'll have to get home by about nine or Liz will be frantic.'

Chapter 3

This is me, folks! Alice Mary Lucas. And I'm in this glitzy apartment in the centre of Rome. It's on the seventh floor and outside there's a balcony the size of a suburban garden with huge earthenware pots of geraniums (or petunias?) white and pink, and two white metal (not reproduction plastic) tables and six really comfortable lounging chairs. From the balcony there's a superb view of St Peter's and all the rest of beautiful Rome, dusky pink and sinning.

As well as the balcony, there's a huge bedroom with a Caesar-sized bed, a marvellously vulgar carpet with fat pink roses and blue true-lovers knots' on a mushroom-soup-coloured background, blue and pink silk wallpaper and a stunning emerald-green silk bedcover.

There's also a huge luxurious bathroom and a kitchen with a fridge full of Soave and Frascati and plushy white peaches (a luxury variety rarely seen in Britain in spite of the EC).

All this is, naturally, the Wages of Sin.

Sins (Sins and Lovers): there are many sins, but I'm not a Catholic – or anything, really – so I haven't a clue which are mortal and which relatively unimportant and rather fun.

The Seven Deadly Sins seem medieval and quaint by this time. I mean, Sloth, for instance. What sort of a sin, I ask you, is Sloth? I mean, if you're totally blanked-out and immobile, at least you're not plotting to blow up planes, making deadlier and deadlier chemical weapons or amassing huge fortunes from cheap, black labour.

Anyway, I love quizzes, so I'll see how I rate on the Big 7.

Sloth:	No. I can't wait to start each day.
Envy:	Definitely not. I pity everyone else.
Gluttony:	Yes. Luckily I'm 5′9″ and do a lot of aerobics so it doesn't show.
Wrath:	No. I'd love to lose my temper and roar, but I'm quite unable to.
Pride:	Yes. Why not?
Lust:	No. While no stranger to hot sex, I don't think I'm quite in the Lust Stakes.
???:	I can't offhand remember No. 7.

So do I get to Heaven? If not, this apartment is the next best thing. I can sunbathe on the balcony without being stared at – what am I saying, I love being stared at – and have delicious picnics without having to share my favourite things or eat other people's lousy sandwiches.

My Favourite Food Everyone has an interest in food, but with me it's an obsession.

Pizza Blanca Oh, this is gorgeous and bears little resemblance to English pizzas. It's really more like crispy fried bread.

I don't think I ought to continue, because my taste in food is simple and peasant-like, at variance with the sophisticated image I'm trying to project.

Appearance Provocative and sexy, especially in my new gear. I have been asked, and this by an Italian photographer, to model some of Umberto Arrizi's Autumn collection. (No, I'd never heard of him either, till I was shown a double-page spread of his clothes in the current *Elle*. He's pretty fabulous.)

Anyway, I've suddenly acquired two pairs of Victorian-style lace-up boots, two pairs of trousers tight as leggings, a white zip-through circular dress and, pride of the collection, a stunning midnight-black jacket, the leather supple as silk, soft as peach-skin.

And how has a newly graduated student like me managed to amass such a wardrobe, you may ask. And you'd be right again!

My lover and benefactor is very rich and moderately famous. He owns and runs an advertising agency (London-based) in which I have obtained a lowly but fairly well-paid position starting next month. He is not quite a sugar-daddy, though at thirty-six, pushing on that way. He has a decided paunch, though he goes jogging every morning – even here – and doesn't eat bread or pasta or any of the truly delectable foods. He hasn't yet lost his hair, but he studies it several times a day as the prophet the stars, the financier the share index. He has many vulgar traits, e.g. a massive gold chain round his neck, monogrammed silk shirts and crocodile shoes, but luckily I love vulgarity in all its most brazen forms. (That's why I'm going to be such a success in my chosen field.)

A wife and a few kids would normally be enough to make me hesitate for at least a few days, but this guy has a wife and an ex-wife, with two children and a nanny apiece, and since they all seem to be leading wonderfully exciting lives in various exotic sun-spots, I had absolutely no scruples. (Well, perhaps I did, once, when one of his sons, Rory, came on the phone and sang to him. 'Why did he sing to you? It isn't your birthday, is it?' 'No, he's just learnt a little song, that's all.')

I never had a father. He was drowned in a swimming accident before I was born. I wonder if I'd have rung him up to sing to him? No, we'd probably have had a very stormy relationship. I'm too like him, according to my mother. All the same, I sometimes feel the tiniest bit deprived.

My English teacher at school, Ms Sheila Burton, M.A., had firm views on the advisability of dragging in a quotation, such as 'The river glideth in its own sweet way'; 'Loveliest of trees the cherry now'; or 'The man's the gaud for a' that and a' that' into every piece of writing.

> *Quotation*
> So, come kiss me, sweet-and-twenty
> Youth's a stuff will not endure.

I wouldn't mind meeting Rory, the singing boy, but I don't suppose I ever shall. Small sigh. Don't think I haven't got a heart.

I've spent many a happy morning alone on this balcony while my inamorato is seeing clients and making deals.

A Roman Tale
Across the road there's a roof garden, which, being on the top of a six-storey block, I can look down at.

Among an array of plants like the Chelsea Flower Show, there's an ordinary washing line with sheets and towels and shirts and underclothes; very incongruous it seems in the centre of Rome. There are also some garden chairs and usually a beautiful young man of about twenty.

I spend much of my time looking at him, and he, an open book spread out over his miniscule briefs, spends much of his time looking at me.

But we both wear identical, black, fifties-style sunglasses; we never smile, have never, in any way, shown that we're aware of each other.

Once or twice two other people, both women, have joined him in the garden, but only to bring out more washing. One is very elegant, dressed in simple navy-blue dress and white sandals, undoubtedly a Beauty, but

24

something about the line of her shoulders, and her elbows perhaps, suggest that she's at least forty. His mother? The other is in her late fifties with an overall-type garment and a cotton scarf on her head. Yet not a maid. It's she, for instance, who decides where the clothes shall hang and which are dry enough to take indoors. It's she, also, who dead-heads the flowers, looking over the plants in a proprietorial way and watering one or two.

Are they mother and son staying with Grannie?

As the two women leave the garden, they exchange a few words with the boy. I imagine them urging him to go on with his reading – he's probably a student, I tell myself, perhaps having to re-take his examinations after a misspent academic year – but he doesn't. He only lies back and watches my every movement, watches me eating a pear and a peach and a honey-cake, watches me, as the sun gets higher, spreading Ambre Solaire on my shoulders and my breasts.

I wonder what would happen if he arrived at my door?

Quotation
So, come kiss me, etc.

A few days ago, our unconsummated affair reached a climax of sorts. The forty-year-old woman came out to the garden on her own, and without any washing. Whereupon the lovely boy drew her down to him and mounted her! Bloody hell! It was over almost before I could turn my eyes away. When she got up, she smoothed down her dress, touched his mouth with her fingertips, smiled at him indulgently and left.

Whereupon he went on staring at me, and I, inwardly trembling and not a little discomposed, went on staring at him.

The End.

My lover, Charles Hamilton, having gone to join his wife in Ibiza, announced – under the impression that I would be feeling slighted – that I was welcome to stay on in his apartment until some friends take it over sometime next month; I immediately bethought me of my sole surviving parent, her straitened means – due to her having recently bought a new and rather undistinguished English car – her hunger and thirst for culture and wine, and decide to phone her, inviting her to join me here.

God, she's had a lousy life. First, my father's death, after only a few months of marriage. Then *My Birth*, to hell things up even more. And as soon as I was five and started school, did she sit back and relax? No, she immediately went off to University, working really hard to get a good degree and rushing home to me every weekend, instead of trying to squeeze in a bit of the old social life. (She wasn't bad-looking when she was young.)

Anyway, after graduating, my mother got a job, teaching English at the local Comprehensive, and within a few months had fallen desperately in love with the headmaster of the school, one David Noel-Smith, and he with her.

How appropriate, how convenient, how jolly, you may think; but you'd be totally wrong. Because David Noel-Smith, like my close friend Charles Hamilton, was a married man.

There the resemblance ends. David Noel-Smith (hereafter referred to as David) was honourable, uxorious and dreary, and hummed and haad for about three years before taking my mother to his bosom, and even then, I've heard whispered, only did it, or did IT, because his wife, Laura Noel-Smith (hereafter referred to as Laura Noel-Smith) had a heart condition and couldn't.

When I was eleven or twelve, my mother confided a little of this to me, assuring me that she placed great trust in my discretion.

All the same, I was sent to a private school, in case my well-known desire to hog the limelight ('I'll tell you a secret. Mr Noel-Smith comes to our house and has sexual intercourse with my mother') should get the better of that frail plant, my discretion.

The affair lasted for God knows how many dreary years.

Anyway, without going into too many boring details, it all ended badly and sadly, and ever since I've wanted to do something for my Sole Surviving apart from taking her morning tea on Mother's Day when I happen to be home, and giving her an African violet on her birthday. And what more suitable or nicer, than inviting her to Rome, and at such little cost to her or me?

I phone her, eager to hear her excited response.

Alas, she is once again in the depths of despair.

She accuses me of being hard-hearted to an ex-boyfriend. My behaviour towards him, she says, has driven him mad. Wait for it. He has been accused of *Rape*.

For once, I am speechless. On two counts.

1. I have treated this boyfriend with exemplary and most unusual consideration, even to the extent of continuing our relationship on a platonic footing – and there is nothing so boring and dreary and dead as dead love and platonic whatsits – but this I bore for at least two or three months because of his insistence that it was the only way he could recover.

   Recover? I resented the implication that I was a sort of disease he was suffering from.

2. Rape. He, Peter Venables, seems the last person in the world I would associate with violence of any sort. He's a wimp. He wears aertex vests and carries his money in a plastic purse. He's a pathetic old woman.

Clearly, I have to return to England. He's lost his mind and perhaps I'm the only one who can testify to this. He's apparently blacked-out all that sunny summer afternoon, all those hours I spent informing him, over and over again, that he and I were finally through.

Me:	You'll forget me all the sooner if we don't meet again.
P.V.:	I don't want to forget you.
Me:	It really is the only way out. All I've succeeded in doing these last weeks is make you more unhappy. A clean break is the only solution.
P.V.:	It's no sort of solution.
Me:	I'm afraid, Peter, that it's the solution I've decided on.
P.V.:	It's no sort of solution.
Me:	This way, you'll get a chance to forget me.
P.V.:	I don't want to forget you.

I should have phoned somebody, there and then. 'Please come to certify this madman,' I should have said. Who – or whom – do you contact, though? Perhaps I should have phoned everyone: the doctor, the Samaritans, the Citizens Advice Bureau, his father, the vicar. (Only his father, the vicar, wouldn't have deigned to speak to me. Once, in the days when I thought Peter a dumb but handsome hunk, I rang him at his home to invite him to a party, and when I gave my name, his father immediately put the receiver down. Could he tell from my voice that I was a Bad Lot? When I hear myself on tape, I think I sound terribly, terribly 'refained'.

Aug. 24th 20.00 hours At Leonardo da Vinci airport, having managed to get a ticket for the next flight at 2100 hours – and thereby spending all the lovely lolly Charles left me.

I didn't at all want to leave the love-nest.

However, I make the best of things, strutting about (gorgeous leather jacket slung over one shoulder, white satin trousers so tight they make my bum look like two hard-boiled eggs) trying to look like an International terrorist trying to look like an International model. I take quick, furtive glances over my shoulder and then, as though nervous about giving the game away, go into a little-girl act, simpering coyly.

Damn! I'm not searched at the barrier! Damn!

A blonde stewardess, her face pink, oval and smooth as a sugared almond, welcomes me aboard. (How I'd hate to be an English rose.)

Mine is an aisle seat. A plump, middle-aged man offers me his window seat. I accept.

When we're airborne, plump man offers to buy me a drink. 'Iced soda please,' I say, speaking through my teeth, abstractedly and a little abruptly, like someone with a bomb in her hand-luggage.

By the time they come round with a snack, though, I'm so hungry that I have to abandon the game. 'Any extra bread rolls?' I ask the stewardess in my normal robust voice. (This is a useful ploy, usually resulting in one being showered with extra packets of baby-sized cream-crackers, triple-wrapped soft cheese, custard pudding, coconut cake and eau-de-cologne fresheners.) Plump man offers me his bread roll which I accept before taking possession of the aforementioned packets of assorted goodies.

I eat my way through everything but the wrappings, finishing off with two cups of coffee with delicious artificial cream.

Plump man says he envies me: tells me he has a weight problem. I try to look surprised.

The guy sitting across the aisle who's talking animatedly to his wife/girlfriend/companion and running a practised eye over me at the same time, is beginning to get on my tit-ends.

I've had enough of all this double-dealing. I write him a note: 'Sorry dear, but I only do straight massage nowadays. Anyway, you know my number if you want to get, as it were, in touch. Love Carleen.' which I shall drop at his feet when I go to the john.

Then, my pen still in my hand, I happen to look out of the window, and instead of the blank, black nothingness I'd expected, there's a breathtaking sunset. Not at all over the top and messy; orange, pink and sulphur-yellow, but pearl, aquamarine, turquoise and the deepest evening blue and so beautiful that I want to shout.

For a moment, I want to be an artist. (My mother begged me to do Fine Arts rather than Graphics, but Graphics, I told her, is what leads to *Money*.) For a moment, though, I want to be an artist, even a poor, unknown, starving artist. Why am I bent on distorting rather than creating?

Oh, I look into the great vaulted night and despair.

I'm suddenly appalled at what's happened to Peter. Because in his dim and blundering way, he's a good person. He's kind and dependable. He cares about old people and whales and nuclear waste. He worries about my life-style, about my not having a mackintosh and not getting enough sleep. He hates it when I get drunk and steal ashtrays and toilet-rolls.

Perhaps he really believed I'd marry him one day, although I told him repeatedly that I didn't intend to. Perhaps he thought I was a good girl at heart and that one day I'd settle down and learn to iron shirts and read computer manuals. Oh Peter, what have I done to you?

'And to your left,' the pilot announces, 'you can see the lights of Paris.'

I tear up the note I've just written into about sixty pieces.

Chapter 4

As I leave Dilys's, I can see a woman standing on my doorstep. As I walk up the path she turns to look at me. She's large, with untidy, greying hair.

'Mrs Lucas?' she says. 'I'm Eileen Venables. Peter's mother.'

I feel my stomach lurching. I unlock the door. 'Come in, please. I hope you haven't been waiting long.' (My mother is also called Eileen. Trust me to be thinking of that.)

'Not too long.' Her voice is nasal and full of misery. Please let her be accusing, vindictive, threatening; anything but sad and timid. If she cries, I'll cry. And I won't be able to stop. And I don't even care about Peter, damn him. I'm on the other side.

I take her into the sitting-room. She sits down, but at the very edge of a chair, managing to look even more uncomfortable than when she was standing.

'Please don't offer me a cup of tea,' she says. (This is no social call, she's saying. As though I don't know.)

'Peter thought he was in love with your daughter,' she says, talking very quickly as though she wants nothing but to get it over with. 'But his father and I told him we couldn't see him until he was free of it. We know your daughter, you see, or at least, know of her.'

She's going to be nasty. Good. I decide to ask no questions, to do nothing to help her.

'I'm afraid, though, that I do need a cup of tea,' I find myself saying. 'I'll have it in the kitchen and come back to you.'

That was neat, I tell myself, as I fill the kettle.

But the next moment I feel ashamed to be playing games at such a time. I decide on a glass of Perrier. I put a bottle and two glasses on a tray and go back to the sitting-room.

'You'll have a glass of water?'

There's a pause; a long pause and then a swallow. 'Yes, please.'

It's a humid, sticky day.

We drink deeply without looking at each other. She dabs at her mouth with a large whiter-than-white handkerchief. If I'd seen her in a railway compartment or in a department store, I'd know she was a vicar's wife; it's the peculiar blend of humility and self-righteousness, innocence and awareness they seem to possess.

'My third son, James, is at Sussex University,' she says. 'He knows your daughter, knows of her, knows her reputation.'

I incline my head, trying to appear cool and unconcerned.

'And he tells us that she's frequently in the company of a *much older man*.'

Simple words, but she manages to hint at such depths of depravity.

'She's got lots of friends,' I say. 'She's very popular. I'm sorry you think badly of her. In fact, she's rather . . . rather . . . a lovable girl.'

A bit wild, but certainly lovable.

'She's been the cause of my son's downfall,' she says.

And then she bursts out crying. She cries openly like a child, with a great slush of undignified noise and looking very ugly, her face red and shiny.

I can't help liking her.

'Rubbish,' I say, after a decent pause. 'She's only a girl, only twenty-two.'

She shudders, almost losing her breath. I wait again.

'Your son has only himself to blame. I've begged and begged him to accept that it's over between him and my daughter.'

She finds her handkerchief again and rubs at her already blotchy cheeks as though polishing brass.

'Would you like to stay here tonight?' I ask.

She opens out her handkerchief, studies it, and has a good, serious blow. 'Thank you, no. I have to go back to the Police Station by six. Then I have to get the train to London.'

She's managed to pull herself together. Well done.

But when she gets to her feet, she looks altogether too much the virtuous, hard-working vicar's wife, mother of five, in her best ten-year-old clerical-grey suit; altogether too much the injured party.

I can't take it.

'I'm afraid I can't feel any sympathy for Peter,' I say. 'You see, I've spent most of the day with my friend, who's in a very bad way, very hurt and frightened.'

Her eyes flash at me, pale and hostile. 'My son tells me she's an actress,' she says.

'Yes, that's right.'

'My son assures me that—'

'That she led him on. That she wanted it. That it was her fault.'

'Yes.'

'I don't believe it for a minute, but I'm glad you do. It will make things easier for you.'

She's no longer childlike. Suddenly she conveys an impression of power and size, her shoulders are broad as a man's.

'You don't believe it?' she asks, her head turning towards me so that I'm conscious of her strong thrusting chin and her strong neck. I can understand something of Peter's admiration for her. I can even begin to understand how she refused to have anything to do with him while he was seeing Alice; only a very tough spirit could be so unwise. I wonder if her husband is as tough? Or altogether milder and meeker? At any rate, I hope he's thanking God for his nice quiet Sunday in Church.

'You don't believe it?' she asks again, as though willing me to confess to at least a shadow of doubt.

'No. It isn't in her to cheat. If she'd wanted sex, even for one moment, she'd have willingly taken the consequences. I'm sure your son managed to deceive himself into thinking she wanted it, but that was his blunder. And a stupid and unforgivable blunder in my opinion.'

She sways a little, reaching out to touch the back of the chair. And I feel sick again, at having to be so blunt.

'Peter's been living here with you?' she asks then.

'He's been staying here for some weeks, yes.'

'Could I go to his room?'

'Of course. He was in my daughter's room.'

'You allowed that?' Her eyes blaze. Pale blue eyes, beautiful, but diamond hard.

'She's twenty-two,' I say. 'I was a widow with a two-year-old child at her age.' (A bid for sympathy. At the very next opportunity, I'm going to get in the bit about my husband getting drowned before my very eyes. Why should I be feeling so defensive?)

'They've searched his room,' I say, wondering if there's anything she wants to remove from it – though what, I can't imagine.

She crumbles again.

'Why did they do that?'

'They'd probably be looking for things that could connect him with . . . well, with other rapes.'

She sits down again.

'They wouldn't have found anything,' I say, as I go back to sit opposite her, 'but I suppose they have to check.'

She opens her large black handbag and looks inside, examines one or two things I can't see, and then brings out, oh my God, a photograph, and hands it to me. It's a studio photograph of her in her prime, a baby in her arms, and four small boys, two on each side of her. The biggest boy is unmistakably Peter. He's about seven, very earnest-looking with large ears.

I'm furious about the unfair advantage she's suddenly got over me. The last thing I want is to have to visualise Peter as a seven-year-old with sticking-out ears.

34

I push the photograph back at her. My eyes are stinging and the back of my throat feels raw.

'He's always been such a responsible boy,' she says. 'Being the eldest he was probably pushed too hard. I expected him to be sensible and helpful when he was little more than a toddler.'

'What's the point of all this?' I ask, getting angrily to my feet. 'We all make all sorts of mistakes.'

'Peter tells me that your daughter became pregnant and that he was anxious to do the right thing by her. But, being so long without hearing from her, he's been tormented by the thought that she might have had an abortion. You don't think that's possible, do you?'

It's an effort to drag my mind from the grave child, the school tie, the too-large blazer. 'I suppose it's possibe,' I say. 'That is, if she ever *was* pregnant.'

'She's the sort of girl who could countenance that? Even after being offered marriage?'

I try not to think of the obscenities Alice would have come out with if she was 'offered marriage'.

'I don't think she'd want to get married,' I say.

'But abortion is a sin against God. Don't you agree?'

I don't answer her.

Having had an abortion myself four years ago, I know they're not the easy, painless solutions that the anti-abortion lobby seems to imagine.

She's disappointed at my lack of moral fervour. Her eyes suddenly narrow. 'Peter's always tried to tell us what warm and wonderful people you and your daughter are,' she says, 'so unconventional and serene and free.' (She sings the words. How she despises us.) 'But he's changed his opinion by this time, I can tell you.'

I still hold my tongue.

'He told me today about your long-standing affair with a married man,' she says. 'Your daughter's headmaster.'

Christ Almighty. It's hardly bearable.

'The headmaster of the school where I teach,' I say smoothly.

'Alice went to a different school . . . But why is my life under scrutiny? I'm not on trial.'

I suddenly have to get rid of the woman, hurt and pathetic though she is. I take a deep breath. 'I think it might be as well if I phone for a taxi now. To take you back to the Police Station. There's nothing more to say.'

I dial the number, make the necessary arrangements.

And then we sit in our corners watching each other.

At least she's got a husband to go home to, I'm thinking. I picture the Vicar, Ronald G. Venables, at Evensong. A distinguished-looking man, according to Peter, with greyish hair and a short beard, almost white. He manages to finish *The Times* crossword every day; is fond of cooking – finds kneading bread particularly therapeutic – hates buying new clothes; is nervous of the dentist. It will be difficult for him to take the Services today but I'm sure he has unquestioning faith in his son's innocence; after all, unquestioning faith is what he goes in for. I expect he'll meet his wife at Euston station later on, draw her arm through his, tell her he's proud of her. At least she'll have that.

They'll go to bed together afterwards, savouring that companionable privacy; two people shut off from the family, the parish, the world.

They've been married for twenty-eight years.

What is she thinking about me, I wonder, as she sits there gazing at her knees. What will she tell the vicar about me? Does she think I'm hard and dangerous? Fast and loose? To someone as drearily decent as I am, the idea is mildly cheering.

We say nothing to each other until the taxi arrives.

Then I go with her to the door and watch her leaving, getting into the car in such an awkward and ungainly way that I feel sorry for her again.

She doesn't smile or even look in my direction.

I go back to the sitting-room and lie face downwards on the sofa. David, I whisper to myself. Oh David, David, help me.

'A long-standing affair with a married man.' How dare she use that in her tirade against Alice? Could I help it that he was married? Long-standing? It was over in a flash, in the blink of an eyelid. What's twelve years out of a lifetime?

Anyway, it's over, it's over. Isn't that punishment enough?

I try to concentrate on something else: Alice. Alice. How indignant she was when I accused her of being careless of Peter's feelings. She'd rung up wanting me to come to stay with her in Rome. She was intent on describing the wonderful apartment she'd been lent for a week, but I couldn't concentrate on it.

'What's the matter, Mum?'

'Alice, it's Peter.'

'Peter?' (I can almost feel her making an effort to adjust her mind.) 'Peter? What about Peter?'

'Love, you should have let him know.'

'Let him know what? That I'm in Rome?'

'That you're through with him. He's been out of his mind expecting to hear from you.'

'Mother,' (now she's offended) 'what can you mean? I spent a whole bloody afternoon telling him I was through with him. I let him plead and argue, even let him shout at me and cry. Because I thought I deserved it. Because he's the sort who thinks the first kiss means marriage and three kids, and I should have known it. Oh Mum, how could you think I'd leave without . . .'

So the poor boy is mad and unaccountable for his actions. I feel a wave of relief washing over me.

She's still talking, but I cut through it. 'You'll have to come home, love, as soon as you possibly can. He's obviously gone right out of his mind. I mean literally, Alice. Alice, he's been charged with rape.'

There's a long pause, so long that I'm afraid she's been cut off.

'I'll come on the next flight,' she says then. 'I'll phone you from the airport.'

'He's been here ever since you went away, insisting that you'd promised to be in touch with him, that you'd promised to phone him here.'

Another long pause.

'Will you be able to meet me? You won't feel up to it, will you? Do you think Dilys might?'

'Ring me from Rome airport as soon as you know the time of the flight. I'll get someone to meet you.'

She's coming home. Alice is coming home.

Why do I start to think of that time when she disappeared in Selfridges during the Christmas rush? When she was about five. I can remember the little coat she was wearing: delft-blue, and the duster-yellow tights. I remember some kind PR man trying to calm me: they'd find her. I wasn't to worry. She'd be in the toy department. She'd be in the Elves' Grotto. She'd be in the crowd of kids around Father Christmas. They'd find her.

And I knew they wouldn't find her in any of those places, because we'd already been to them all, twice each. And the PR man wouldn't let me join in the search – I must have been in a terrible state. Oh, and the dazed relief when someone finally brought her to me. She'd been at the make-up counter trying to buy me a Christmas present with some money I didn't know she had. 'They were showing me rubbish,' she complained, as she tried to wriggle out of my arms. 'Plastic boxes with soap in. I didn't want to give you rubbish.'

There's a tap at the door. It's Ralph. He walks straight in, as he always used to.

(It was a Swiss hand-embroidered handkerchief that she'd finally decided on. She had a penny change clutched in her hand.)

'I lost Alice in Selfridges,' I explain, in case he should think I'm always in tears.

Many men might be disturbed (Alice? Selfridges?) but Ralph, who'd lived with Dilys for three or four years, takes it all in his large, policemanly stride.

'Tell me another time, love,' he says. 'I'm already late and Liz will be getting franctic. I've got three things to tell you, right? One: I've been down to the station and given the Chief Detective Inspector my view of the case. Two: they've let the bastard out on bail – a thousand pounds surety from his mother – while they decide whether there's to be a trial. Three: I'm taking Hywel home with me, so please remind Dilys where he is if she suddenly misses him.'

'Thanks for coming, Ralph. It was a great help.'

To my surprise he bends down and kisses my cheek. (The egg and chips, I can hear Dilys say.)

'See you soon,' he says . . .

'Ralph, come back,' I shout just as he's getting into the car. (What do I care about Liz? Being frantic is the normal state of mind of a policeman's wife. I've watched enough television to know that.)

'I haven't told you about Alice,' I explain, as he walks back towards me.

I see him hesitate, probably uneasy in case I'm going to ask him to go and look for her in Selfridges.

'She's in Rome,' I say, to reassure him. 'She's just phoned me and told me that Peter knew perfectly well that it was all over between them. Had known for weeks.'

'So there was no possible excuse for his behaviour. Is that what you mean?'

'No. I mean it shows that he's completely deranged . . . Doesn't it? I mean, to let me think he knew nothing at all. For all that time.'

He becomes stiff and cold. 'Come off it, Sarah. You're not going to be a witness for the defence, are you? You keep that deranged bit to yourself. As far as I'm concerned, he's the bastard that raped my wife . . . I mean Dilys. Right? And I'll never forgive you – and neither will she – if you start making excuses for him. You believe her, don't you? That she was raped?'

'Of course I do.'

'And so do I. She's given me all sorts of hell, but she's never told me a lie – it's not in her nature. She was raped. And that's the end of it as far as I'm concerned. And I want the bastard that

39

did it in jail for ten years, not writing poetry in some nice mental hospital.'

He gets into the car, glares at me, slams the door and drives off.

I go back to Dilys' to see if she needs anything. She's paler than ever.

God, what a day. Nothing but worry. About Dilys. About Peter – damn him. At least Alice is coming home, that's something. That's a great deal.

However did she get the apartment in Rome? The rich man-friend, of course; 'the much older man' Peter's mother mentioned, her voice and expression managing to suggest vice, drugs and a deserted wife or two.

Alice's headmistress used to say she'd go far. Was this what she meant?

Chapter 5

I've always seen Sarah as the victim, myself as the strong one; I've always been the strong one. Other people have car accidents, burglaries, devastating illnesses, but I go on unscathed, picking up the pieces, sorting through the debris, visiting the hospital. Good old Dilys.

Well, this time it's my turn and I can't bear it. I feel so used, so humiliated, limp as a rag doll.

I've done everything I can think of to help myself: relaxation exercises, deep breathing, yoga, but I still want to scream. Every time I think about him; the way he moved in on me, that terrible smile on his face, I want to kill him.

And afterwards, looking at me so insolently.

And telling the inspector and that dim policewoman that I'd been, 'Oh yes, a very willing partner.'

They believed him, of course. 'How old are you?' the policewoman kept asking me, two or three times at least. 'Forty-three in October.' 'I see. Forty-three next birthday. And are you married, single or divorced?' 'I'm divorced.' 'Living alone at the moment?' 'With my son.' 'Who happens to be away from home this weekend?'

Everything is loaded against me. I want to scream. I can't bear it; the frustration. I'll put on that damned relaxation tape again. Or shall I just scream?

I'm young, just out of drama school, just beginning in the theatre. My life is so rich, so full of promise. I can't stop smiling because I'm so happy to be alive, to know I'm going to be a great actress. To others I may be only a pretty *ingénue*, but I know I'm going to be great, really great. I take in everything around me, savour and hold on to every moment of truth and revelation. I'm learning, learning. Not only technique, but how to be someone else, how to express sadness, joy, emptiness.

That wonderful director we had at the Sideshow: Tanya Anderson. She taught me so much, how to sit absolutely still but letting the emotion I was feeling take over my face and my hands and my whole body. She said I was promising . . . good . . . very good. She taught me to concentrate on all the smallest details which together give a performance subtlety. She used to say that every emotion you tried to express was enormously complicated, that nothing was completely good or evil. 'Are you lonely?' she used to ask me. 'Right. Feel it. Use it. Make it work for you. Are you happy? Right. Get to know it. Use it.'

'Every experience can enrich you,' she used to say. 'Are you disappointed in love? Dejected? Heartbroken? Good. Now you can begin to imagine what real suffering means.'

I was so happy at Drama School and in those first two years at Birmingham. So full of hope and promise. Where did it all go? How did it all go wrong?

When I met Bernard I lost my self-confidence. Being so much in love, I became less ambitious, less thrusting almost overnight. It became less important to get the leading part than to spend even an hour or two with Bernard, I'd miss a morning's rehearsal sooner than miss his phone call. And when we started living together, his career took over from mine. It was as simple as that.

Young women today are not so ready to sacrifice their chances for a man, but I was. I gave up everything for Bernard and he let me do it, probably without even realising it. When I became pregnant and we got married, I told myself that I was only giving up my career for a few years, but it was never the same afterwards. I never believed in myself in the same way afterwards. Love turned me inside out, enfeebled me. That's what being in love meant – to my generation anyway.

I was happy enough. I was madly in love and I think Bernard loved me back. He couldn't be faithful to me, but I think I was the only one he really loved.

I suppose I was too demanding. Brought up as I was in a big noisy family in a small terrace house surrounded by other big noisy families, it became second nature to fight for what you considered your rights. And I fought for Bernard's love, for all his love and all his attention, and couldn't put up with less. If only I'd been able to put up with less. 'He bade me take life easy. As the grass grows on the weir.' He'd been brought up so differently; in a quiet, dignified middle-class home where no-one ever shouted and stormed, no-one made any demands. 'But I was young and foolish. And now am full of tears.'

Poor Bernard. After the first meeting with my family, my father and mother, my grandmother, my three brothers, my five uncles and their wives, my three aunts and their husbands, all my cousins and poor Auntie Lottie, he never expected me to be completely normal.

They loved him so much. Because he was going to marry me, I suppose, because he was going to do the decent thing and make an honest woman of me, and me four months pregnant and an actress besides. They laughed at everything he said and clapped him on the back because he was a middle-class socialist who knew nothing about real life and admitted it. 'Our Dilys's intended,' my Uncle Ifor announced in the Lion with unconcealed pride and all the lads and even the older men crowded round to shake his hand and offer him a drink and ask his opinion on all the most weighty subjects they could think of because he was a cameraman and worked on the telly. He managed to evade most of the questions, though his stutter grew more and more pronounced as he tried to keep up with the Saturday-night revellers. And when I got him to my aunt's at last – there was no room for him in our house – he passed out in her best bedroom, slept until three and refused to eat anything for the rest of the day. This, though, instead of being seen as a sign of weakness, only added to his reputation. 'Dilys's young chap, you should see how he treated Auntie Eva. No-one's ever managed to escape one of her breakfasts before, but he just said, "No thank you, Eva," and kissed her hand and she just simpered and let him off. There she stood with her frying pan full of best back, couple of eggs, mushrooms, fried potatoes, sausages, but there was no contest. Poor Uncle Les, he'd be alive now if he'd only managed that firm, "No thank you Eva," and the little bow. We've got a lot to learn, boys, no doubt about that.'

Our wedding day a fortnight later. Oh, I can't bear to think about it, not in the state I'm in now. It was one of the worst days of my life, though Bernard quite enjoyed it, I think; the endless speeches, all the hot embarrassment.

God, the blessed moment when we finally got away. To that small hotel high up in the Cotswolds. Early February. The wind whistling outside, the lights spluttering, banks of flowers in the hall, the smell of pine cones and wood fires. And Bernard undressing me very slowly and laying me on the bed and stroking my stomach which was already swelling a bit and putting his ear to it, saying 'Is that my family in there?' I've never forgotten that; so full of love and promise.

We didn't do much. Brisk ten-minute walks in between rain storms – the skies were spectacular, vast and threatening – which gave us an excuse for yet another bath together and yet another tumble in the king-sized bed. Apart from that, all we did was sit close together on comfortable old sofas, reading our horoscopes in posh magazines, yawning and giggling and having morning coffee and afternoon tea while waiting for our very delicious meals.

I'd never felt so united with anyone, so much at peace.

How could it have lasted? It was too wonderful to last, too much of heaven for this world.

Oh Bernard, you didn't manage to forsake all others, did you?

Not even for that first rotten year. What a mess it was, all the lies and the rows.

If only you could have taken the trouble to be a little more careful. If only I could have been a little less anxious, a little less obsessive. If only. If only.

And the saddest thing is that we still love each other, still need each other, still phone each other at least once a week.

If he was in London now instead of in Turkey or Cyprus with Tom, I might ring him up and tell him about that monster who raped me; the policewoman who thought I was lying; the bloody doctor who was so cold and unsympathetic. And his voice would thicken and he'd stutter a bit and he'd say, 'Listen, I'll come up. I'll get rid of Denise/Isabel/Francesca/Mary Louise, get into the car and be with you in a couple of hours. OK?'

And he'd put the phone down and I'd start to shiver because I'd be waiting for him again. No, I can't do that. I'm not going to choose that way ever again.

I married Ralph so that he'd stop me crawling back to Bernard. I never loved Ralph, not really, so I deserved all I got, even that hiding he gave me when I told him it was all over. (That's something I never even told Sarah, just stayed in bed until I could walk again, told the boys I'd fallen down the stairs; I had bruises just about everywhere.)

Anyway, if I hadn't married Ralph, I wouldn't have had Hywel, so it was all worthwhile, I suppose. Strangely, I seem to love Hywel more even than Gareth and Tom. Even though he looks so much like bloody Ralph. Bloody Ralph! How could I have married him? He held my hand yesterday, trying valiantly to feel some sympathy with me, but dying to ask which dress I'd been wearing, the one with the cleavage or the one with the frill instead of a skirt, and thanking God for Liz. Liz isn't too bad, not for a policewoman anyway. I wish she'd have a baby though. Hywel would love it.

I had a really bad labour with Hywel. Sarah was over with me keeping me company. The boys were in Wales with my mother. I'd had a picture postcard from her that morning, 'Boys very happy. Please send vests.' Where was Alice? Perhaps they still had that Nanny. Anyway, Sarah was very keen to contact Ralph. Because I was making so much fuss, I suppose – I don't believe in suffering quietly – and the midwife had left saying she'd be back in three or four hours. Three or four hours, when I didn't feel I could bear another three or four minutes, and I kept on saying, 'It isn't Ralph I want. I want Bernard. It's Bernard I want.' And I remember her leaning over and asking me very solemnly, 'Is it Bernard's baby, Dilys?' 'Of course it isn't Bernard's baby. It's Ralph's bloody baby, but it's Bernard I want with me. Is that so difficult to understand?'

She didn't know me very well at that time. She thought I was just confused and delirious.

But at last she was so frightened by all my sobbing and pleading that she did ring him up.

He wasn't in, though. Perhaps it was just as well because I know he'd have come if he thought I needed him, and bloody hell, I needed him.

Anyway, when Hywel was born it was all right again and I tried to put up with all Ralph's joy and excitement and even managed some of my own. Hywel was lusty and beautiful within minutes of being born.

All the living I've done. All the laughing and crying. What's it all for? I'd really like to be able to use it, Miss Anderson. I really would like to work again.

Perhaps I could sell my share of this house to Ralph so that he and Liz could live here instead of in the police flat they've got now – they could easily commute from here – Hywel could live with them and I could move back to London and try and get a job with some fringe theatre group. Have I got the guts to do that? Get some tiny flatlet and have to struggle again to make ends meet? Be the oldest in the company instead of the youngest? Playing the nurse instead of Juliet?

Could I do it? After so many years of taking things easy. Looking after Hywel, helping him with his homework, sorting out his rugby kit, taking him to Scouts and Youth Club and all his matches and practices; being here for Gareth and Tom and assorted girlfriends during their holidays; making Sarah little comforting meals when she's particularly tired and letting her cry on my shoulder; shopping and cleaning, with feet up at frequent intervals for cups of tea and the *Guardian*. Not an unpleasant life, but what does it add up to? Being in a comfortable cage, I suppose, a cage of my own making.

Couldn't I break out? Hywel could come for the weekends. I wonder what he'd think of the situation. Gareth and Tom would be proud, I know. They're always saying I should do something worthwhile again instead of slacking here and going up to London for the occasional advert. I don't know about Hywel though. Or am I using him as an excuse for staying here?

If I could become really independent, people would have more respect for me. And I'd have more respect for myself. The need for love puts you down, the dream of being married and taken care of. Can't I take care of myself by this time? Can't I put the past behind me? Can't I forget the way I was brought up?

In our house, my father toiled underground, his work uncomfortable and physically exhausting, so that at home he was king, fed like a king and pandered to, not expected to do anything except go out to the pub every evening. On Saturday he took my mother out to the club which was her big night and all the social life she aspired to. She seemed entirely satisfied with life because she'd got a good, dependable man. My father gave her the larger part of his pay packet – good money – she shopped, cooked, looked after four children, kept the house spotless and visited and helped my grandmother and some of my great-aunts. It seems to me that she was satisfied with too little, but perhaps that's true wisdom. For a woman, I mean.

I was always so scathing of Sarah's love affair, but it was all she wanted; those few hours her precious David could spare from his busy life and his sick wife. She always managed to convince herself that she was the luckiest person alive. She was in love. Wasn't that enough?

If only I could have been satisfied with less than everything.

Perhaps if I'd had a Nanny and kept on working and been able to devote even half my energies to my job, I wouldn't have demanded so much of Bernard. At least he wouldn't have had my undivided attention. Perhaps no relationship can stand up to undivided attention.

If I went back to London, to that poky little flat and that demanding job with a fringe theatre group – which would probably be called 'Injury Time' or 'Howling' or just 'The Company' – it wouldn't be altogether impossible to start seeing Bernard again.

Could I do it?

Chapter 6

Still waiting at the airport. No-one meeting me, though I phoned Mum from Italy, as requested, to give the arrival time.

I've also rung three times from here, but there's no reply. Where the hell is that woman at this time of night? Doesn't she know I worry about her?

I have another coffee.

I have no money for a taxi and there's no other transport.

No chance of anyone taking me for a terrorist now. I've just caught sight of myself in the mirror; I'm looking younger and more pathetic by the minute.

I try to read a colour supplement which I've just picked out of a litter bin. Nothing but adverts for horrid kitchens, one with twenty-five cupboards. Do I really want to spend my life trying to persuade people that they want a kitchen with twenty-five cupboards? Imagine looking in twenty-five cupboards for the Kenco.

Absolutely nothing worth reading. Articles on Sellafield, Prince Edwards, and the Church in Russia.

'Basil, lemon, peppermint, clove, rosemary, sage, fennel. I was once told that repeating that twenty times induces a feeling of soporific calm. After saying it half a dozen times I feel like dashing my head straight into a wall.

49

Why is it that no-one comes to chat me up when I really need it?

As usual when I'm feeling lonely and depressed, I descend to a fantasy world, a stupid adolescent daydream.

A man, that's what I want! A man who's intelligent and generous and very sensual, who loves talking and walking about the streets and who makes me laugh. He needn't be very handsome or very rich and certainly not charming – a very suspect quality in my opinion.

What if he came through those swing-doors now? 'Excuse me,' he might say, 'but can you possibly give me a 10p for the phone?'

'Of course.'

I give him one. (A widow's mite. It leaves me with about nothing.)

'Thank you so much.' He's looking at me properly for the first time.

'Can I buy you a drink?' he asks. 'After I've made the call? Or are you waiting for someone?'

'No, I'm on my own.'

Oh, that wonderful moment when eyes meet and breath quickens. That first kiss, that gasping, drowning sensation. Oh God, why can't those trembling feelings last at least a month or two?

Was it really like that for me and Charlie? I honestly think it was.

We met back in the spring.

The chap who'd interviewed me for the job – Douglas Holmes? Donald Holmes? A cold fish, anyway, though civil enough, I suppose – had taken me round all the offices and workrooms afterwards, introducing me to various people, heads of departments, and so on, and had finally walked me back to the reception hall. 'We'll be in touch within the next few days,' he said. 'Thank you for coming.'

I just managed a tight-lipped smile. The interview had gone badly. I was feeling sick about the questions I'd failed to answer, the bright things I might have said. At the beginning I'd even been nervous! Me!!

As I went down in the lift, I felt like banging my head against the wall but, as there was someone standing behind me, I worked off my frustration by doing my squint.

'Hey, you'll stick like that,' the person behind me said.

Noticing the mirror in front of me, I spun round to face him. He was someone I'd been introduced to in the last hour, but I'd already forgotten his name.

'That's better,' he said. 'That's much, much better. What the hell was wrong?'

'I wouldn't work in this bloody place if they went down on their knees to me,' I said, enunciating each word slowly and clearly.

Being almost exactly the same height, we were eye to eye, and when the lift came to a stop and we were jolted, very nearly mouth to mouth.

In that second, I knew he was going to offer me a drink or a meal, or his hand in marriage or something. What he did was press the lift button so that it went straight up again.

'This way,' he said, when it stopped and the doors opened.

I followed him through a large room full of drawing-desks and people working, into a small inner office. After closing the door, he got a bottle of champagne from a fridge and poured us a glass each. 'Miss Lucas,' he said, 'I'm not going down on my knees to you – at least not this afternoon – but I have great pleasure in offering you the job you applied for.'

I love champagne. 'Thank you,' I said, taking a large gulp.

'And since that's settled, could we move on to some other business?'

At that moment, he still hadn't touched me, not even with the tip of his little finger, but I'd been knocked flat by a ninth-wave of passion; my nipples were sore, my tongue swollen.

We swayed towards each other and kissed. How long does that sort of kiss last? For that space of time, it seemed like something I'd been waiting for all my life. And the second kiss was even deeper and more abandoned. When I looked into his eyes, he seemed like someone drowning. And during the next kiss, I felt I was drowning too.

'We're not going to do anything here,' he said, after that third kiss. 'I'm going to take you home now. We've got plenty of time. We don't need to rush things.'

But anyway, I started to pull my clothes off, in case he changed his mind. And after a while he did.

We had some good times. So many rich people are mean as hell, but he'd got a flair for spending. Once he sent me five hundred white narcissi. (He gave me a diamond pendant, too, but I wouldn't take that. That sort of thing lays claim on you.) He also gives large sums of money to charity; and even if it's only to ease his conscience, plenty of people don't.

So why have I become rather bored and dissatisfied with him? Why am I already casting around for someone else? Why was I relieved when he went off to Ibiza yesterday? God, I never thought it was pure love or anything like that, but surely even impure love should last three or four months?

It's not that I don't like him. He's OK. He worries a lot about his children, for instance. His daughter had to have a tonsils operation a few weeks ago and, my God, you'd think it was a pioneering liver and kidney transplant from the fuss he made. 'Listen, I had my tonsils out when I was a kid,' I told him, 'and it's honestly not too bad. It's a bit painful the first day, but they give you ice-lollies to suck and by the next day you're ready to go home.'

It didn't do any good, though. He felt better only after he'd managed to find her a miniature Gucci watch and sent it off to her by express delivery.

He certainly loves giving presents. When he bought me this coat he was more excited than I was. 'Is it calf?' I asked him. 'I've no idea.' 'I suppose you just asked for the most expensive coat in the shop.' 'It wasn't a shop, it was a showroom. And I didn't have to ask for what I wanted. They knew.'

God, it's absolutely typical of me to be spending my time thinking about Charles Hamilton when I should be tearing my hair and wearing my brains out worrying about Peter.

Rape? What are they on about? I can't think of anyone in the world less likely to descend to any sort of violence. His favourite words are obedience and authority. He apologises to lampposts when he bumps into them; he lets anyone, even crippled old women, push in front of him in queues; he doesn't like pubs if they're crowded and noisy; he's much too nervous to join any demonstrations. When I lived in a tree outside Newbury for three or four days, he thought I was a martyr though I was having a great time. He won't even say a word against the Church.

Rape? Perhaps it's a case of mistaken identity. Oh, why do I have all these problems? One moment trying not to feel guilty about Charlie's bloody wives and the next having to worry about Peter's problems, though they're nothing to do with me. I'd told him a hundred times that I wasn't going to see him again and he lets Mum think I'd gone off without letting him know anything. Perhaps he's mad.

Chapter 7

Alice gets her strong physique and vivid good-looks from her father, Geoff. To be honest, I don't often think about Geoff nowadays. We were only married for just over four months.

Occasionally I look at my wedding photographs, at the handsome man by my side, and realise that I can hardly remember him. In each of the pictures he and I have blank faces, even when we're smiling we look neither happy nor unhappy.

Only our parents seem happy. Or at least relieved.

My parents were in their late thirties when I was born. They'd been childless for years and I'm certain they didn't want me; I don't just mean before I was born, but at any time. They always treated me kindly, but rather as they might have treated a refugee from a different culture, whom they strove to tolerate but couldn't hope to understand. Any love they had to give was only to each other.

Before I went to school I spent most of my time with a series of au pairs, but not one of them stayed with us long enough to make much of an impression on me. They came for a year and seldom stayed any longer, one of them was so homesick that she left after only three months.

When I was six I became one of about half a dozen day pupils at a small private boarding-school. Day pupils were never completely accepted; perhaps this was the reason I was never happy at school, always feeling that some essential bonding took place after I'd left at four o'clock.

When I was a teenager I read, studied, played the piano and listened to the radio – other people had television but we didn't – and occasionally went to the cinema. I had no close friends, but even if my parents had noticed, they would have had no idea what to do about it. I stayed at school until I was eighteen.

Though I had decent A level results, no-one suggested that I should go to College or University. At that time most privately educated girls seem to be satisfied with some short, fairly useless course when they'd finished with school: cookery or modelling or something of that sort.

So, bored with living at home, and still feeling that my parents were happier without me, I settled for a year at a secretarial college in Hampstead.

Before the end of the first week I'd moved out of the ladies' hostel someone at Church had recommended to my parents, having managed to get a tiny room in a top-floor flat in Belsize Park. (*Three girls invite fourth for super pad NW3. Own room. Share expenses.*) I remember being very excited as I shopped for towels and sheets in John Lewis's before moving in; it was better than a birthday.

The other girls, two Catherines and a Jane, were friendly enough, but once again I was the outsider; they'd been together for almost a year. I was only a replacement for a certain Arabella Hudson who'd taken herself off to Paris. They lived full and exciting lives while I stayed in listening to music and washing my tights.

What energy they had! The minute they got back from work they'd be dashing about in bras and pants, washing their hair, waxing their legs, ironing their Laura Ashley dresses, which had been on the floor behind the sofa since the previous night, or even the previous week, making urgent phone calls to men called Julius and Marcus like Roman Emperors, and coming in at two in the morning, banging doors and filling the flat with a heaving perfumed excitement.

'Want a coffee, Sarah?' they'd occasionally call out, possibly unaware that I'd already been in my small hard bed for almost four hours.

They'd often invite me to parties, but I was always too dispirited to go. Though I was slightly younger than they were, I felt like a maiden aunt. They were used to London, the rush and noise; in my worst moments I feared I'd never get acclimatised.

And in spite of all my early nights, I wasn't doing well at college; my typing speeds were lower than average and I detested shorthand. I often considered leaving, but what else could I do?

One Friday evening, feeling depressed by the oncoming winter – I remember a chill wind blowing from the Heath and the leaves of the lime trees dropping down like large yellow tears – I stopped at a small shop opposite the underground station and bought myself an attractive but odd-looking dress that I happened to catch sight of in the window.

Some burst of confidence made me show it off to Catherine, Catherine and Jane, and they overwhelmed me by their shrilling approval. It was super. It was fab. It was me. In it I looked like Marianne Faithful, Susan Hampshire, Julie Christie. I was finding myself. I simply had to come out with them that very night. There was a party at Dot and Justin's. I needn't worry about an invitation or about taking a bottle. All I had to do was put on some eyeshadow and be ready by nine o'clock.

So, a new purple dress (blueberry, the woman in the boutique had called it), plain but figure-hugging, gave me the confidence to go to a party that weekend, and at that party I met Geoff. It was as simple as that.

Geoff was older but less ebullient than the Roman Emperors. Perhaps he was a bit of an outsider too; he'd been in London for six years, but his home was in Birmingham and he'd arrived at University from a grammar school. He had a strong presence, a definite standing in the company, but I felt that he'd worked for it, rather than achieved it by some God-given right. I know I liked him far more than the men my flatmates brought home, who shouted at one another instead of talking and brayed with laughter at their own inanities. In Geoff's company I found myself relaxing.

And he fell in love with me, or so he said. Desperately, or so he said.

It certainly gave me something to think about. Suddenly the week's typing marks didn't seem of such overwhelming importance.

No, I couldn't persuade myself that I was in love. What I felt for Geoff didn't begin to measure up to the love I'd long been reading and dreaming about.

I'd been Silvius in our production of *As You Like It* at school: 'It is to be all made of sighs and tears; And so am I for Phebe. It is to be all made of faith and service; And so am I for Phebe. It is to be all made of fantasy, all made of passion and all made of wishes; all adoration, duty and observance; all humbleness, all patience and impatience; all purity, all trial, all obeisance. And so am I for Phebe.'

I felt little of this for Geoff.

All I felt was pleased to be sought out and admired by him. I also felt more important than I'd ever felt before: I suppose I was simply very happy to be loved, and settled for that.

Geoff certainly had some of Silvius's attributes and what he lacked in the sighs and tears section, he more than made up for on the passion and impatience side.

I wasn't mad to get married, but Geoff was – he was twenty-six – and since I wasn't mad to do anything else, it seemed an easy way out.

Out of that noisy flat, the hectic life-style, the secretarial college with its weekly progress charts.

I took Geoff home for Christmas. My mother, Eileen Dukes, amateur pianist and assistant WVS area organiser, seemed to like him; he was good-looking and not too much of a provincial. My father, Desmond Dukes, bank manager and very little else, thoroughly approved of him, because he was a chartered accountant with a promising job in the offing, whereas the sons of many of his colleagues were selling their motorbikes and guitars and going to India in beads. We had an enjoyable few days together.

Geoff took me to his home for the New Year. His father owned a factory in Birmingham – making nuts and bolts – and his parents had a massive house in Solihull with a sunken bath in every bedroom.

Geoff's parents approved of me so wholeheartedly that I was immediately aware of a formidable list of previous girlfriends, stunningly beautiful perhaps, but not made of the appropriate wifely material.

Whereas I was. They approved of my South of England accent, my simple hairstyle, my clothes – lambswool sweaters, pleated skirts, narrow leather belts, all in drab, Jaeger colours. I suppose I had Middle Class written all over me, and that was the label they wanted.

'She's a nice girl who's been well brought up,' I heard Geoff's mother telling some of her friends at the engagement party they gave for us. 'Yes, he's given us some anxious moments, but now his father and I feel we can relax.'

We got married in April, the day sunny and bright. There were two hundred guests and a hundred wedding presents.

My parents gave us a large cheque.

Geoff's parents gave us a large house, brand-new, one of twenty-eight forming a half-circle overlooking the sprawling industrial town where Geoff had recently landed his first job.

It had been the estate's show house, furnished by a well-known firm of interior designers from Knightsbridge, and when Geoff voiced his approval of the furniture and fittings, his parents bought those as well; the thick dove-grey carpets throughout the house, the paler-grey sofas and armchairs, the mahogany dining-room suite, the bronze curtains, the standard lamps, even the cut glass vases on the drinks cabinet, the pictures – mostly in shades of pink – on the walls, the satin hangers in the fitted wardrobes and the luxury soap which exactly matched the towels which matched the tiles in the two bathrooms.

I can't remember what I thought of it all; perhaps I was too busy, too excited, too nervous to do much thinking. By this time, though, I'm left with the hazy impression that I wasn't in quite the same state of euphoria about every single item as Geoff was; perhaps I'd have welcomed a voice in at least some minor matters such as the colour of the lavatory paper.

We went to Crete for our honeymoon, gold labels with Mr and Mrs Geoffrey Lucas, 5 Foxlawn Avenue, Shipsley, Staffs, in thick black lettering attached to all our new luggage.

We stayed a full month, and it was a time of rewarding novelty. Geoff was both ardent and experienced, and I found that I wasn't as cold and awkward as I'd feared I might be; though a complete beginner, I felt I showed some promise.

And success, or relative success, in this endeavour was reflected in others; sight-seeing, sun-bathing, walking on the hills, wining and dining were all pleasurable. We had a happy time.

We hadn't intended to start a family for at least two years, but within a month of our return, I discovered that I was pregnant. (Within another month, Geoff had completely forgotten that the event was unplanned. 'After all, why should we wait?' he'd say to neighbours and colleagues. 'We're not short of money. We've got the necessities of life and a little more.')

'I'm having a baby,' I wrote in my diary, trying to feel calm and responsible and adult.

All I felt was terrified. And very, very sick.

I'd never been ill before. My morning sickness lasted all day and kept me awake at night. I couldn't bear to do any cooking, couldn't bear even to heat up the ready-prepared dishes in my new freezer.

When I was able to eat, I wanted only white bread-and-butter and Weetabix with warm milk. Geoff took to having his dinner at the Swan before coming home from work and once or twice travelled the ninety-five miles to his parents at Solihull for Sunday lunch.

'I can't help it,' I used to say. 'I don't choose to be like this.'

'I know you don't,' Geoff would agree, but looking at me doubtfully.

Only our cleaning lady, a middle-aged woman called Mrs Way, tried to remonstrate with me. 'Come on, come on, it isn't as bad as that,' she used to say, bringing me a cup of tea as I lay prostrate on one of the long pale-grey sofas, 'Put your feet on the floor and you'll start to feel better.' I've often remembered – and acted on – the advice since, but at the time it washed over me like another wave of nausea.

This stage of my life lasted eleven and a half weeks.

Within a few days of its being over, I discovered that Geoff was being unfaithful to me.

I found a folded-up scrap of paper in the pocket of a suit he'd asked me to send to the cleaners. 'I don't mind if you are married,' a certain Sandra D. had assured him in a large childish scrawl. 'You're such a wonderful lover. I dream about your big cock.'

I felt giddy with shock; the bedroom seemed to be tilting, first one way and then the other, as I stood staring at the nasty little note.

Why hadn't he torn it up and got rid of it? Was he proud of it? Was he keeping it as a testimonial? Was he a wonderful lover? I had no way of judging.

When the giddiness subsided, I was filled with a furious energy and after packing up the suit and disposing of the letter, went all over the house, polishing the furniture already kept highly polished by Mrs Way. What should I do, I asked myself.

The thing that really confounded me was the extent of my anger and jealousy. Why was my mouth dry, my heart burning, over someone I was fairly sure I didn't love?

I tried to assess my position. I had a wife's status. I had a fine house full of expensive furniture and all the latest gadgetry, huge wardrobes with sliding doors to hold the clothes I was encouraged to go out to buy, a nursery to plan, a social life to aspire to. I had a large solitaire diamond ring and a string of beautifully matched cultured pearls.

However, I wasn't sure how much I wanted all these grand acquisitions. In one way or another, they'd all cost too much. I'd recently discovered the unsavoury facts about cultured pearls; that they're obtained from oysters artificially impregnated with the irritant which eventually produces the pearl.

A good wife is a jewel of great price, according to Solomon – or Confucius – or one of those other boring old patriarchs.

A good wife is an imprisoned oyster, I thought, as I polished and fumed. I imagined myself secreting the silvery slime, which after forty years of unremitting irritation becomes the jewel of great price, or at least that pretty counterfeit, the cultured pearl.

'God, you're looking so much better,' Geoff said when he came in that evening, proceeding to hug me as he hadn't done for weeks. 'You've got colour in your cheeks and a sparkle in your eyes. Let's go out for a celebration meal tonight.'

'It's because I'm angry,' I said.

'It suits you,' was his reply, as he pulled me down on to the sofa, imprisoning me again with his desire, his male smell, his long limbs.

Yes, you are a wonderful lover, I thought later. You must be. My anger had turned to a vaporous feeling of relief that I didn't have to take any immediate action.

All I had to do was to get suitably dressed up for a meal in a smart restaurant. I still felt hopelessly confused about everything, but the worst of the pain had been kissed better.

I remained confused. For all that Geoff reiterated that I was the love of his life, his beautiful doll, his child-bride, his meat and drink, his apple pie, his reason for living.

When he made love to me, I sometimes fantasised that I was Sandra D., thirsting for his kisses and his . . . large . . .

How absurd love was. How could anyone take it seriously? I didn't love Geoff. Or did I? I certainly loved the hardness of his body, the triangle of black hair on his chest. However much I mocked the idea of being in love, I felt the strangest flutterings in my stomach as I watched him getting undressed and climbing into bed.

He had a few days off and decided that I'd benefit from a short stay in the seaside town in Dorset where he used to spend his holidays as a boy.

It was the last week in July. I was still thin, but my breasts were noticeably larger and I had a small hard swelling at the base of my belly. I'd begun to take iron and vitamin tablets and was trying to work up an interest in baby clothes.

It was cold stormy weather.

On the last day of our holiday, he took me to a small cove, five or six miles from the town where we were staying; it was associated, in his mind, with sunshine and cream teas and cricket on the beach.

On that day, it was almost deserted. Two small boys with pale-blue anoraks and pale-blue faces were building a fort in a narrow strip of sand, while their parents were taking a brisk walk up to the headland.

I settled myself in a sheltered spot among clean blue boulders and announced that I was going to have a sleep. I was happy. Afterwards I remembered the feel of it, salt on my lips, my body languid from after-breakfast love.

Geoff leant over me. His eyelashes were dark and thick, his eyes a pale-grey with a hint of yellow. I'd got to know that moment when they narrowed, became blurred, like blind eyes.

I laughed him away. 'Leave me alone, you. You know how tired I am after that hike you took me on yesterday. Leave me alone.'

The children had finished their castle and were now most happily demolishing it, bashing at it with their flat wooden spades. They took a few flying kicks at the mound of sand that remained and then went running up the cliff path after their parents.

Geoff watched them for a moment, then turned towards me again. The cove was quite deserted.

I struggled to sit up. Geoff had pulled his shirt off and in the cold wind, his tanned body had taken on a sinister, purplish tint. 'Sarah,' he said, in the thick voice I'd got to know so well.

'I don't want to,' I said.

'Don't be a prude.'

I felt my heart beating and a surge of warmth travelling up my body; all the same my overwhelming instinct was to fight.

'I don't want to,' I said again.

'Yes, you do. You do.'

'Tell me about Sandra,' I said, just as his mouth was about to close over mine.

He drew away.

'Sandra D.,' I said, coldly and clearly.

I hadn't intended to cause him such pain. He looked as though he'd been physically assaulted, as though someone was pushing a knife into the small of his back.

'You bitch,' he said, drawing away from me.

I'd had no conscious plan to bring out the name at such a time. It was in no way premeditated. All the same, perhaps I'd been hoarding it away for some such use.

I tried to say something. I wanted to apologise, though surely he – with his big cock – was more in the wrong, but I couldn't get the words out, could do nothing but shake my head.

'I'm going in for a swim,' he said then, wrenching off his trousers.

Oh please don't, I wanted to say, it's far too rough. Oh please don't. Please.

All I managed was small, barely audible, 'No.'

He turned from me and walked towards the sea. I watched him go. His trunks were a shiny sky-blue and the sky was the colour of porridge.

For all these years, I've had to try to stop myself thinking of the rest of that day: my panic, guilt, sorrow.

For the first hour I thought he'd swum to the next bay and was keeping out of my sight to punish me. By the time I'd realised it was something worse and had managed to get help, it was too late.

His body wasn't discovered until high tide that night.

Having to bear the memory of the quarrel we'd had was the worst thing of all; the agonising thought that I'd driven him – not to suicide, I never in my worst moments considered that – but to going for that swim in such a rough sea.

It was years before I got over it. Perhaps I'm still not over it. Whenever I'm worried – as I am now – I can never tell myself that the worst can't happen. Because I know it can.

Chapter 8

Jack Wells appears! Oh, joy! I honestly thought I was going to have to stay here all night.

Mum must have been feeling pretty desperate to have contacted Jack Wells. He's a teacher at her school whom she rather despises. Something about his North Country accent, probably, and his array – or disarray – of strange but colourful clothes. (David Noel-Smith always wears dark suits and ties.)

I like him, though. Dear old Jack. He lives near us. Not in our posh, pseudo-Georgian crescent where even the cats wear fur, but in a rather shabby Victorian terrace down the hill. When I was at school, I used to baby-sit for him and his wife.

He kisses me and says I look cool. (The older generation are rather pathetic when they try to use buzz-words.)

I can't help squeezing his arm though, as he takes me to his car. Such is the effect of two hours of solitude, trying not to consider past follies.

His car is a dirty, F-registration Sierra with a large dent on the near-side wing. (I can't help noticing these things. Aggressively immobile people are the advertiser's nightmare.)

'She was sorry she couldn't come herself,' he said, as he opened the door. (Reflect how a certain class of people – C2 and C3 – are always using pronouns, e.g. ''er indoors', as though referring to someone by a proper name is not quite permissible to people of their humble origin. God, I wish I wasn't such a poxy snob.)

'Do you mean my mother?' I ask.

'Yeh. She was sorry she couldn't come. She's in a bit of a state, what with one thing and another.'

I remain silent while he pays the parking fee.

'I'm not surprised,' I say, afterwards. 'She's had a hell of a shock. So have I. Did you ever meet Peter?'

'Yeh. Twice or three times. Met him with you in the Crown, don't you remember? We had a game of darts.'

'What did you think of him?'

'Bloody hopeless, if I remember right.'

'Come on, Jack. Don't pretend to be thick. What did you think of him as a person? I know you're a good judge of character.'

'I am?'

'My mother says so.'

'Good Lord! And I was under the impression that she thought me lousy at everything.'

'No. But we were talking about Peter Venables. What you thought of him.'

'He seemed under your thumb. He seemed anxious to please. He seemed tense. Would I have picked him out as a possible rapist? Of course not.'

'Quite a long speech, for you.'

'Yeh. But what about you? Didn't you suspect anything? That he had this violence in him?'

'Absolutely not. He was always meek as a lamb with me.'

'She's had quite a time with him. He wouldn't leave your house because you'd promised to phone him.'

'I didn't promise anything.'

'Are you pregnant, by the way? *Were* you pregnant?'

'Certainly not. Rather an impertinent suggestion, if I may say so.'

'Only he said you were. I thought that might be a lie as well. But she was very worried. Particularly since you hadn't been in touch for such a long time.'

I turned to him. 'Oh Jack, I feel terrible.'

He immediately draws in to the kerb. 'Get out,' he says tersely.

'Get out?'

'Yes. If you want to be sick, just get out.'

'I don't want to be sick. What's wrong with you? I'm not a child. I just feel awful about worrying my mother.'

'Oh.'

Silence for a moment. I think he's surprised to find I have any of the finer feelings.

'Only Stevie was sick in the car a couple of weeks ago and the smell's only just going.'

'How is Stevie?' (His daughter. She must be about seven by this time.)

'Fine. As long as she walks everywhere.'

'And Fred?' (His son. About five.)

'Bloody little heathen.'

'You got custody, I hear.'

'Yes.'

'My mother told me. I was very upset. By the divorce, I mean. Lena doesn't look like my idea of a lesbian.'

'She fooled me, too.'

'I'm sorry. Oh dear, did you mind me bringing it up? Actually, my mother only told me that Lena had gone to live with the woman who has the Riding Stables at Bishop's Harvard. I only surmised the lesbian bit. I mean, I'm sure she wouldn't have left you for a horse.'

'Thanks.'

'Oh Jack, you *are* offended. I'm sorry. I shouldn't have mentioned it. I'm an idiot. Will you forgive me?'

'Stop behaving like a spoilt child.'

We travel in silence for some miles. I usually love driving at night; rainy nights, the humming of the engine, the sleepy rhythm of the windscreen wipers; deeply satisfying. Only this time it isn't.

'I am a spoilt child. You're right.'

'Oh, you'll grow up.' His voice has lightened. 'So, tell me about you. Rome, eh? What's that all about? Work or play?'

'Play. Nothing permanent, though.'

'What is permanent?'

I'm suddenly light-headed with tiredness, which makes me tender and sentimental. As usual.

'Has it been bad for you?' I ask, wanting to put my arms around him. Dear Jack. I like him so much.

'Fairly bad. Over it now, though. Over the worst.'

'I never liked Lena much.' (It isn't true. At one time I'd idolised her, bought polo-necked sweaters and pleated skirts just like hers, black patent shoes and Ma Griffe perfume. That was when I was fourteen, fifteen. How long ago it seems. 'I never really liked her.'

'I did,' Jack says.

I can feel tears running down my cheeks. I rarely cry, but to my chagrin, I've done so twice in the last few hours.

'*It's over,*' Jack sings. '*My baby doesn't love me any more. It's over. It's over.*'

He has a most untuneful voice. 'Try the radio,' I suggest. 'Let's have some sloppy, night music.'

One day, I'll settle down with some nice, solid chap like Jack.

But not yet.

Perhaps I'll go back to Rome for another few days before beginning my job and settling down. Charlie said he'd get away from Ibiza for a couple of days, would say that something had cropped up. (Not that his second wife would believe him, after all she'd been the something cropping up, not so long before.)

'I'll tell you who I fancy quite a bit,' Jack says, 'and that's your mum. She can't stand me, though, so what's the use of that?'

I'm too surprised to say a word. Jack's a presentable man; short but compact, his chin kept close to his chest like a boxer. Not much older than Charlie, though certainly more worn and battered. My mother is a different generation. My mother is forty-two or something, isn't she, forty-three or something. Definitely over the hill.

'And I'd be a bit more use to her than that Noel-Smith, I can tell you. But there you are, she's the faithful type, that terrible, romantic type, faithful unto death, and all that crap:

No other Sun has lightened up my heaven,
No other Star has ever shone for me.
All my life's bliss from thy dear life was given –
All my life's bliss is in the grave with thee.'

I never, never thought to hear Jack Wells reciting poetry! In his flat, expressionless Northern voice.

He's supposed to be mocking romantic love, but you could hardly realise it from the way he recites that poem. I have this vision of sweeping moorland and grey tumbling skies and feelings that are very craggy and true.

'Bloody Noel-Smith,' he says then, in exactly the same dispassionate voice. 'Made her a laughing-stock. Everyone thinking they'd get married as soon as his wife died, instead of which he goes and gets religious and has nothing more to do with her.'

'Perhaps he became impotent.' (I'd read somewhere that shock and remorse could cause this. Also mumps.)

'I'll tell you one thing . . .' he says.

But he never does. Because we'd arrived in Foxlawn.

'She's over with her friend,' he says. 'Where do you want to go?'

'With Dilys? Why is she with Dilys?'

Strangely enough, I know the answer before he's said a word: it's Dilys that Peter is supposed to have raped.

'Because it's her he's supposed to have raped,' Jack says. 'I thought you knew that.'

'Why did you say, supposed to have raped?' I ask.

'I've no idea. A slip of the tongue. Go now.'

My mother has come to the door. 'I'll give you a bell in the morning,' I say. 'I'll come over to see you.'

Mum walks towards the car, but Jack waves and drives on without waiting for her thanks.

Chapter 9

Alice arrived at about a quarter to two this morning and though we were both so tired, we stayed up talking instead of going to bed.

Naturally, she's terribly upset about Peter. She intends to try to see him tomorrow or the next day, though what good it will do I can't imagine. (She's feeling very guilty about him. We talked for some time about it. I pointed out that the alternative to finishing with him was marrying him and surely she didn't think she should have done that.)

It turns out that she isn't – and hasn't been – pregnant. That was another of poor Peter's imaginings. I must say that I'm very relieved; having an abortion isn't as easy as some people – Peter's mother, for instance – seem to imagine.

I had one just over four years ago. On the twenty-third of July; the date, and every other detail, is fixed in my mind, and probably always will be.

I didn't tell David anything about it. With his wife so ill, it wasn't as though there was any decision to be made. He thought I was having a routine minor operation. He sent me flowers, pink and white roses, and of course I wept over them, thinking, of course, of what might have been.

I was in a small side ward with an older woman – I suppose she'd be about forty-five – who was having an abortion because her husband had had a serious accident at work and needed her constant attention. She had three grown-up children.

'I would have liked a babby,' she kept saying, over and over
again. 'Lots of women uster have a last little 'un, when their first
family was grown. They uster get a bit spoilt – all their older
brothers and sisters doting on them and buying 'em everything
they wanted – but they usually turned out all right. No, I
wouldn't have minded a babby if things had been different.'

We were both very depressed.

Enough of that. 'I wouldn't have minded a babby if things had
been different.' Enough of that. David never even suspected what
I'd gone through.

Alice won't accept that I can't return to Rome with her in a few
days time. 'Dilys is tough,' she keeps saying – which is exactly
what Dilys says about her – 'Dilys will be OK. She's in a bad
way now, of course she is, but she's the sort who recovers from
things. She'll be all right.'

I wish I were as confident.

She tells me about the man she's been with in Rome. None
other than the head of the Advertising Agency she's going to
work for. She says he's *great fun*. I wish she wasn't having all
these affairs, but at least I'm thankful she isn't breaking her heart
over anyone.

She asks me whether I've succeeded in getting over David and
I have to confess that I still miss him almost unbearably. It's
almost a year since his wife died and he wrote me that letter
telling me he didn't think we should go on seeing each other. '
know that you can understand the grief I am faced with in these
terrible days, what struggle to accept God's will. Even at the
end, when she was too weak even to smile, I kept on urging her
to make one more effort for my sake. I know that I have been
monstrously selfish towards her and you, and I pray for forgiveness. While I am so broken in heart and spirit, I feel I have
nothing left to offer you. I'm sure I can depend on your understanding.' And so on, for another five pages.

I didn't answer it. I didn't know how to. I was pleased that

74

I'd been a source of strength to him, but couldn't help feeling that I'd been something else as well; after all we'd done more than hold hands, and I knew I couldn't have written back without at least a hint of reproach.

For a long time I felt that his letter had been written in an excess of grief and guilt and that he'd eventually be able to accept Laura's death and begin to forgive himself, but by this time I've completely given up hope. (Have I?)

'Tell me, did you used to like David?' I ask Alice. (The first time I've ever dared, she being so blunt and forthright.) 'I used to, I think,' she says, 'but I've gone right off him by this time.' Of course, she's too young to know anything about the unendurable strain he was under for so long.

To my surprise, she suddenly seems very taken by Jack Wells; starts telling me how sympathetic and supportive she found him. He'd recited some poetry to her in the car. Poetry! Jack Wells! The thought chills me to the bone. He must have been trying quite desperately to impress her. How frightful if she went from poor mad Peter Venables to Jack Wells with all his anarchic posturing.

I only just manage to refrain from telling her what a thorn in the flesh I always find him. Not that he isn't kind. Oh, he is. After all, he was the first one I turned to when I needed someone to fetch her from the airport. (I wish, now, I'd got a taxi.)

Even after Alice goes home – at about three – I can't stop thinking about Jack Wells.

He and I have conflicting ideas about everything. We've had furious arguments in the past. I don't know anyone I've clashed with so often. He's supposed to be an English teacher – his degree is in English – but he won't spend half enough time on literature: he seems to think books are elitist. When I insist that English can't be studied without resource to the best writing we have, 'Balls,' he says. 'What we need is less good writing and more good sense. My aim is to teach my kids how to stand up for themselves as future citizens, how to use a directory and a phone and a reference library, how to fill up forms, how to challenge authority whenever they think it necessary. I'm trying to teach them how to talk fluently and write simply.'

Of course, I agree with those aims, but insist that they fall short. But if I make large statements about books being windows on the world, affording insight, for instance, on the intricate relationships between people, he pretends not to understand me.

'Books,' he says. 'What do you know about the type of child I have in my classes? They live in houses where there's only one room that's heated – and that's if they're lucky – and the telly's on, and on loudly, to shut out the sound of anyone knocking at the door for the rent or the HP, so where are they ever going to read a book?'

'But isn't that an even stronger argument for giving them a taste of literature at school?'

'I teach English for everyday life,' he says, 'a plain man's English.'

'Yes, but . . .'

He takes no notice of me. Why should he? I can't help knowing that he works very hard and that his pupils are responsive and outgoing. On a Wednesday morning I happen to be supervising a Sixth-Form private study group in an adjoining room and I overhear one of his lessons in progress.

'Right,' he says as he comes through the door, 'Raymond, I'm Mr Brewer. I'm absolutely furious with you because you've forgotten your PE kit again and you know I'm just about to make you run twenty times round the field in your vest and underpants. Now say something – quickly, quickly – that's going to make me change my mind and send you to the library instead.'

'Mr Brewer, Sir,' Raymond begins.

'Good, Raymond. Firm opening. Carry on.'

'My mother a'nt been well, Sir, and she couldn't get me kit washed.'

'No, Raymond. Poor. You haven't considered who you're dealing with. In any conflict, you must consider your adversary. Trisha, what's an adversary? An enemy? Not bad, but not exactly. We'd better look up the word in our dictionaries. No, we haven't all got one, and we all know why. Share with your partner. All right, one between three. Who'll be the first to find adversary? Martin? An opponent, one who takes up an opposite position. Well done, Martin. So an adversary is not quite as strong a term as an enemy. Right? Now, Raymond, if your particular adversary was Mrs Hunter, Home Economics, who's a fairly reasonable person, I'm sure she'd be prepared to accept that excuse and let you borrow what you needed from someone in another form. But we're not talking about fairly reasonable Mrs Hunter, are we, but about Mr Brewer. Now, who can tell Raymond what Mr Brewer would reply to, My mother wasn't well, etcetera? Raymond? You've had second thoughts?'

'He'd say, Why couldn't you wash it yourself, you lazy pig.'

'Yes. That's exactly what he'd have said. You're thinking now. Once you start thinking, it puts you in a different league, doesn't it? It puts you level with your adversary, your opponent. Never allow yourself to get too frightened to think. Short pause. Think. Right? Who'd like a shot at spelling "adversary" for me? You've all seen the word, haven't you, in the last few minutes. Elaine? Come out to the blackboard then, Elaine . . . Not bad. Not bad. Not exactly right, but a jolly good try. Forget what other teachers may have told you about spelling being the most important thing in the world. It's much better to use the exact word however it's spelled than to make do with a useless little word because you happen to know how to spell it. And anyway, what's the point of being great at spelling if you can't think of anything worthwhile to write down. Knowing how to *think* is the most important thing in the world. Right, you can sit down, Elaine.

Samantha, you've got yourself a job in a café. That's what you want to do, isn't it, when you leave school? Yes, starting off washing dishes and working up to assistant cook. Good. Now, the manageress calls you into the café and starts to tell you off — she's found some lipstick on some of the cups — and in front of everyone. Now, you don't want to lose this job. Remember how difficult it was getting one? Remember all those phone calls you made? All those interviews you went to? So stop and think before you answer her.'

'I'd still walk out, Sir. I wouldn't stand for any old cow telling me off in front of everybody.'

'Well, Samantha, most of us seem to agree with you. Better no job than one where you're humiliated. OK, let's change the scenario. She's come to the kitchen to speak to you, she's obviously angry, but at least she's civil.'

'All right, I'd say, I'll wash 'em again. It must 'ave 'appened in that rush we 'ad yesterday – when you said 'ow quick I'd been.'

'Excellent, Samantha. Quick apology and then a quick defence. And that could finish up with her apologising to you and no hard feelings. The important thing is to think before jumping in to the attack. Now then, Raymond, have you got anything better worked out?'

'Forgot me kit, Sir. Can I wash the car for you, Sir, 'stead of doing PE?'

'Good, Raymond. Now you've assessed your adversary. Quick apology and an offer he can't refuse. Well done.'

His lessons are certainly lively enough: he gets on well with the children he teaches and gives them plenty of self-confidence. But, as I've said, the complete lack of literary content worries me.

I suppose he's equally critical of my lessons. I try – much too hard, probably – to will the children to appreciate at least some part of every play, novel or poem we study. How ridiculous I must sound, day after day, lesson after lesson; my boundless enthusiasm, my near-reverence. 'Listen to this passage. Can you feel how effectively this or that or the other has been dealt with? Can you hear how the rhythm has quickened – like heartbeats – in the last paragraph? How the short words and hard sounds add to the intensity of feeling?' And so on, and so on. Trying to make them understand what I imagine I have understood.

Still, he can't entirely disapprove of my teaching methods,

because he was furious when I decided not to apply for the Head of English post last year, accusing me of putting my private life before the good of the school. (I would have liked the post, but my applying for it would have been an embarrassment for David, at a time when he had too much on his mind. And besides, if I'd got it, there might have been some who'd think I'd worked too hard for it.)

I have another sleepless night. So many worries. I can't bear to think of how changed Dilys is – and of how much she still has to go through. I'm also worried about how much it will affect Alice. She tries to give the impression of being strong and ruthless, but though she's firmly on Dilys's side, I know she was very fond of Peter and won't quite be able to stop herself pitying him.

And however hard I try, I still can't accept the break from David.

I married Geoff because he asked me to, and because, at the time, it seemed a sensible, grown-up thing to do, and certainly better than typing.

I fell in love with David though I knew he was married. It was far from sensible but I couldn't help myself; I felt I was being sucked down into something by forces outside my control. It often made me think of Geoff and the rough sea which had taken him.

I was twenty-nine by the time I'd finished at Oxford and managed to get a job in a local school. David was fifteen years older.

For six months, overwhelmingly in love, I thought he rather disliked me, and wondered why. He seemed far more at ease with several of my younger colleagues. At the parent/teacher Christmas dance, he'd danced with several of them and afterwards introduced them to his wife. He didn't ask me to dance and it was someone else who introduced me to her. Towards me he was always aloof. And because of that, I started behaving in a correct, prissy, school-teacher way towards him. I tried to be different, but I couldn't.

One Saturday afternoon I bumped into him in the town library. It was towards the end of March; my second term at his school was drawing to an end.

I noticed him joining the queue at the counter. I was a few places in front of him, but as it happened, the assistant who was about to stamp my books was called away to the phone and by the time she'd got back, he'd drawn level with me, and we had to walk out together.

'Always rains on a Saturday afternoon,' I said, in what I hoped was a calm, bright voice.

He put his hand under my elbow. 'Cup of tea?' he asked.

I looked up at him. 'Please.'

I knew exactly what I was doing. I can't pretend to have thought for a second that the invitation was anything to do with tea. There was something else in the urgency of his voice, something in that firm grasp of my arm, something in the air.

(Sometime later, he said he'd been trying not to fall in love with me from our first meeting, which was when I fell in love with him. It was at my interview for the job. He was on one side of the table with three other people, two men and a woman; governors of the school. They had asked irrelevant questions in an off-hand manner; he'd asked probing, intelligent questions politely. Not that I'm trying to suggest that this was a reasonable basis for falling headlong in love; it wasn't. Was it his appearance? Hardly. He's no more than moderately good-looking; small and dark with intense clear grey eyes that seem to look through you, into you. When I was recalled later and told that I'd been chosen for the vacancy, I knew that the most important part of my life was about to begin.)

There was a café across the road from the library. He ordered scones and jam as well as a pot of tea, but I was afraid to eat in case I choked. We sipped tea, looked at each other and didn't speak much. He was wearing Saturday clothes, a corduroy jacket with leather patches on the elbows, a check shirt; he looked younger than in his usual dark suit. He asked me about Alice, I remember; how old she was and whether she looked like me, managing to make it sound as though it was a condition to be most earnestly desired.

I think we must have spent about an hour in the café. We parted at the door; our cars were in different car-parks. 'Shall I see you again?' he asked me. 'I come to the library at about four o'clock every Saturday,' I said, and we looked at each other calmly and with complete understanding. I didn't have to spend a week wondering whether he would be there. I knew he would be. I knew that something momentous was beginning, something that everything else in my life had been leading up to.

I told Dilys about it on that first Saturday.

I remember going to her house – Alice, ten, was at a party on the other side of town – and finding all the family, except Ralph who was on duty, at their evening meal. Hywel was in a high chair, a solid, blond, baby policeman. Gareth and Tom, the sons of a film cameraman, were entirely different types; dark, small-boned and highly-strung. I poured myself a cup of tea, helped cut up Tom's baked beans on toast, then took over Hywel who was having bread-and-butter soldiers dipped in soft boiled egg. (If I looked away for even half a second, his sharp new biters reached the tips of my fingers, seeming not the least averse to the taste of human flesh.)

When I'd managed – during the quieter parts of 'Dr Who' – to tell Dilys my news, she only sighed. 'For God's sake, Sarah, think what you're doing. I've nothing against your going out with a married man who's tired of his wife and ready to give you a good time, but this guy's got a sick wife he's devoted to. Where does that leave you? Having a rotten time with a miserable, guilt-ridden man, only too ready to take it out on you. You deserve better than that. Tell him you've had second thoughts, that you've come to your senses. Oh Sarah, for God's sake, just tell him to go to hell. I feel sorry for him, I really do, but he's got no right to implicate you in his personal problems.'

I looked at Dilys pityingly. How little she knew of love. Ralph, her second husband, was a steady enough man, but as unexciting as Tom's baked beans. I hardly knew her first husband, Bernard, but according to her he'd spent most of his time running after girls. Had she really loved either of them?

She seemed to assess a man by how good a time she could have with him, whether he'd be able to take her to shows in Town and to wine and dine in expensive restaurants.

I, on the other hand, was trembling with excitement, stunned, bowled over with happiness, at the thought of having a Saturday afternoon cup of tea with David and being allowed to share his problems. I was so much in love with him that I'd settle for anything.

'Don't you think you deserve something better, some chance of happiness?' Dilys asked, as though reading my thoughts. 'You seem to be intent on sacrificing yourself. For God's sake, Sarah, the thought of you starting an affair with that sad, defeated man gives me the creeps.'

Of course, nothing she said made any difference.

We were very discreet, seldom meeting except at my home, and that only for a few hours once a week, but he was hardly ever out of my mind.

School was something to look forward to, because I saw him there. We'd meet by chance in a corridor, on the terrace, or in the library; sometimes when there was no-one near. 'How lovely you look,' he'd whisper. At other times when there were children and teachers milling past, we were only able to glance at each other without even smiling, but the look he gave me was enough to melt my bones. The sound of his voice, the touch of his hand made me shiver . . .

I think it was almost two years before any hint of our affair got about. Madge Morgan, the school secretary, was the first to discover anything, and she was a known gossip.

'Oh, Mrs Lucas,' she said one afternoon when I went in to the office to hand in some report cards. 'Mr Noel-Smith asked me to give you this note.'

Was she looking at me rather knowingly? I tore the letter open to let her see how unprivate it was and read it in her presence. 'Sorry, my love, can't make it tonight. I'll ring at nine. D.'

'Whatever is it, Mrs Lucas? You're white as a sheet. Sit down for a minute, do. Shall I get you a glass of water?'

'No, no. It's nothing. It's nothing.'

I could think of no excuse. I wanted to leave but had to stay because I felt so faint.

He came in as I was still sitting there. 'Whatever's the matter?' he asked. 'Mrs Morgan, could you slip out to make Mrs Lucas a cup of tea?'

I was furious with myself. 'David, she'll guess that there's something between us,' I said. He went on holding my hand and stroking it.

'Then she'll be right,' he said calmly. 'Then she'll be right, won't she?'

I told Dilys about it that evening. 'Why should he worry?' was all she said. 'After all, nobody's very likely to carry tales to a sick woman. But why the hell did you get into that state? Was it simply because he couldn't come tonight?'

'No. Oh no. You see, I had a premonition of it being over. Of another letter I'll have from him one day.'

Chapter 10

Last night Sarah insisted I went to bed early with two sleeping tablets and a cup of cocoa made with milk, a disgusting drink that makes you ready to die not just sleep.

'After twenty minutes you'll drop down into a lovely dark pit,' she told me. I wasn't sure I wanted to. It sounded weird. I wouldn't let her leave me.

So she said she'd read me some of Shakespeare's sonnets while they took effect. 'Number thirty-three,' I said.

I wanted the same one over and over again.

'Even so my sun one early morn did shine With all-triumphant splendour on my brow . . .'

'Again,' I kept saying. 'Again.' I suppose I was shamming really, like when you pretend to be much more drunk than you are, so that you can get away with shocking everyone. She was getting a bit tense by the fourth or fifth reading. And then, sure enough, I sank down into the dark cavern she'd described. They were the first sleeping pills I'd ever taken.

The only drawback was that I was horribly awake again four hours later. I heard the front door open at two o'clock and Sarah whispering as she let Alice in. I heard them in the kitchen, opening the cupboard and the bread bin and the fridge and getting the cups and saucers from the dresser. Every sound seemed magnified; I swear I heard Sarah tipping the instant coffee into the cups. Then they went into the sitting-room and I could hear them chatting. (I wished I had a daughter. Sons are all right, but they don't chat.)

I suppose I'm pleased that Alice has come home. It shows her concern I suppose. But who is she concerned about, Peter or me? I know she's fond of Peter. That was the problem. It's easy enough to dump someone you dislike, but when you're at all fond of him, it's trouble.

Will she believe that I was raped, or will she be ready to think that he just blundered on a bit further than I'd meant him to, and that I over-reacted? She's more critical of me than Sarah is. That's natural enough.

I wish those sleeping tablets had an amnesic effect. I'd like to have forgotten everything that happened. If only the hideousness was completely wiped out of my mind, I wouldn't have to take any action. I don't at all want to go through a wretched court case. I can't stop thinking of all the people who'll be ready to think the worst of me. Because of my age – past it – with two marriages and two or three affairs behind me. If it had happened to Sarah, people would be prepared to be sympathetic, because she looks what she is, a warm-hearted, innocent, unworldly teacher, and I look what I am, a desperate, attention-grabbing, out-of-work actress.

If I was quite sure of winning, I don't think I'd be so determined to fight. But because I'm in such a weak position with everything stacked against me, I feel I must make a stand. Sheer cussedness, I suppose.

'Yes, I was dressed in a very short, tarty dress. Yes, I've had two husbands and several lovers. Yes, I'd invited him back to my house knowing I was alone there. Yes, I'd given him a double whisky. No, it was not what I deserved. Because I knew him – thought I knew him – and liked him; considered him a fool, but at least a civilized fool. No, I was not even slightly sexually attracted to him. Yes, it's quite possible that I might have wished to console a young man crossed in love, but not that particular young man. Yes, it is possible that he was under the impression that that was my aim, but what I'm asserting is that he didn't test that assumption by making some tentative advances, but simply pinned me down on to the sofa and raped me. No, I wasn't at all passive. Everything I could do, I did, but he's a very large, strong young man. I pushed him under his chin so hard I thought I might break his neck, but it didn't stop him. No, I've never been raped before. Nor assaulted nor even sexually humiliated.'

I was answering the judge's questions until dawn.

'Go up the mountain,' my Gran used to say when anyone in the family, or in the street, had a problem. It was the only place around us where you could have privacy and quiet. It was a good place, lovely in summer; larks and the rushing sound of brooks and little waterfalls. I tried to think about that mountain behind our house . . .

I remember having a wonderful day up there with a boyfriend called Owen. Owen Gregory. We'd bunked off school. I had my lunchtime sandwiches and he had a couple of packets of crisps and a big bottle of lemonade. After a long ramble, completely alone, we took our shoes and socks off and paddled in a swiftly-flowing stream. Previously we'd only kissed in the dark warmth of the cinema; it was quite a different sensation to fondle and kiss standing in bright sunlight and in a rush of very cold water. I remember surprising myself with a sudden urge to take all my clothes off as I stood there with him, realising how exciting it would be to have him cupping cold water over my naked belly and thighs . . . I didn't, of course. I was only fourteen or fifteen, hardly old enough to be kissing, but I remember the surge of warmth spreading between my legs and wondering if this was how temptation felt. Lead me not into temptation. Did Owen feel the same? For a few seconds he pressed me so hard against him that I could hardly draw breath, but then he became even more excited about a buzzard flying immediately overhead and the moment passed.

The sun dried and warmed our feet, we finished the lemonade; the bottle, dripping love, passing from one to the other, and then we put on our shoes and socks and started walking again.

'I'd never marry anyone who didn't have a small waist,' Owen said as we parted. It seemed some sort of declaration.

When I got home, I rushed up to my attic bedroom, took all my clothes off and measured my waist. Twenty-one inches. My breasts were round, my hips narrow, I had freckles over my nose, my legs and feet had caught the sun and I knew I was ready for love.

Owen and I drifted apart, though; I was on the look out for someone older and more experienced. I wanted love – sex – but I wanted it to be as perfect as that first intimation of it. Any boys who made passes at me thought I was frigid, but I was only waiting. I waited over three years.

The summer when I was almost eighteen, I spent a week in a little seaside town in West Wales with my cousin Mali. One evening when we were watching the annual regatta, we noticed a handsome American college boy watching us. He gradually edged closer and when the last race was over, asked us to have a drink with him, and of course we accepted. We found a table in the garden of the nearest pub and sat looking out at the sea, the little bobbing boats and the darkening sky. Or at least he and Mali did. I looked at him; his skin tanned and moist, his beer-coloured hair curling a little at the neck, his wide mouth, his sleepy eyes. I wanted him.

He and Mali talked about Paris, I remember. He could hardly believe that I'd never been there. 'But it's only a couple of hours from London,' he said. I'd only been to London for one afternoon, but of course I didn't say so. I don't think I said anything, only listened in a kind of swooning trance, to him and Mali talking about Picasso and Matisse and Braque. And waited.

When the pubs shut at last, he said he wanted to go for a walk on the cliffs and asked us to go with him. To be truthful, I think it was my cousin Mali he was more interested in; she was a voluptuous twenty-year-old. But when he disappeared to find the lavatory I told her how much I fancied him and she very kindly remembered a previous assignation and made her excuses. So that I had him to myself. And about an hour later he had me. He was surprised that I was a virgin; I was so ardent, I suppose. He kept on saying, 'Wow,' I remember. At first I thought he wanted me to stop what I was doing; it was almost exactly what my Uncle Ben used to say to the ponies underground, but then I realised it was an exclamation of approval and carried on.

Mali and I were going home the next day, but I told him I was going to Drama School in London in a couple of months and he wrote down my address on his arm and promised to contact me, but he never did. Perhaps I wasn't as good at love-making as I thought I was – I'd read quite a lot about it by that time, but perhaps one needed more than theory.

Perhaps, though, he had a bath that night, sponging the address off his lovely golden forearm before he'd realised it; Americans are always bathing. I never saw him again anyway, but I often thought about him. Wow!

Physical love has been such a delight and excitement and balm over the years, sometimes all three; but now it will always be spoilt, poisoned. I remember a spoonful of apricot jam I was given as a child after a particularly vile dose of penicillin. I was never able to stomach apricot jam after that. And it used to be my favourite.

Gran didn't believe there was such a thing as mental suffering. If you had enough to eat and a roof over your head, you should count yourself lucky. And if you could manage to get out to the shops with a few pounds in your purse, you were among the blessed. Yes, there was a time to mourn when someone had died, but there was also a time to give up mourning, and that was even more important. As far as anything else was concerned, it was a matter of pulling yourself together and refusing to feel sorry for yourself.

She'd have no sympathy for me. She'd be with that bloody police inspector all the way. 'Wasn't it very largely your own fault?' She always knew best, or thought she did.

After my grandfather's death, she lived with my Uncle Ifor and my Auntie Mary Ellen and their three daughters, but she kept an eye on all of us. She'd had seven children, all brought up very strictly and all a credit to her she used to say. Her five sons had gone down the pit and both her daughters had married colliers, but she didn't want or expect anything else. They all lived locally, were all healthy and good-looking, they all called to see her at least once a week and all deferred to her. I suppose she had quite a happy life: she went out shopping every morning, bullying the shopkeepers, most of whom she'd known as children, into giving her the best of everything at no extra charge; she helped in the house and the garden; she had a stream of elderly ladies calling for cups of tea and a gossip every afternoon, and on Sundays she dressed up in her black with the fur and went to chapel and sang hymns.

She couldn't reconcile herself to the sixties and seventies, though; all her grandchildren wanting to go away to College and University instead of getting married and settling down. My eldest cousin, Gwen, slipped away to Cardiff to train as a nurse without too much opposition, but when another cousin, Rhian, won a major scholarship to Oxford, Gran really started fretting and sulking. She didn't care how much of an achievement or honour it was, young girls met their doom among all those upper-class people in those heathen places; came back either pregnant or debauched with black circles under their eyes and chains round their ankles. She begged them to heed her words. (In fact, the outcome was far less exciting; Rhian got a First and became an archivist.)

My mother was almost afraid to admit that I'd got a place in a Drama School in London, but Gran took that news very quietly. London was a place that Welsh people, even decent Welsh people, had been going to for decades: there were Welsh chapels there and Welsh clubs and male-voice choirs. She herself, didn't we remember, had a first cousin who kept a Dairy in St John's Wood, which was a genteel place full of doctors and bankers. Anyway, I'd be all right anywhere, she said, because I was so fit. My mother was upset, I remember, because 'fit' was only another word for common.

My other grandmother had died before I was born. Her

90

husband was killed in an accident underground when she was still in her early twenties, leaving her with three children, the eldest of them my father. Somehow she managed to get a few months' training in a local hospital and became the village midwife. I'm supposed to take after her in appearance.

I never managed to find out much about her, though I often studied the photograph of her which was kept on the mantelpiece in the front room. I thought she looked smart and rather important in her uniform, her little round hat pulled down over her forehead.

Only once did I overhear my parents talking about her. I think my father must have said something about her being particularly clever or superior or hard-working which hadn't gone down too well with my mother, because she suddenly said, 'When she died, there was a rumour that she was pregnant. Did you ever hear that?' 'Good, God,' my father said, 'what are you talking about? She was over forty by that time and if she'd have had any man hanging around her, I'd have been the first to know. Pregnant indeed! She had cancer of the bowel. It was on the certificate. You saw it.'

'I know,' my mother said, a little too smoothly. 'But there you are, people will say anything around here. And that Dr Williams was always calling on her for one thing or another. And he was quite handsome in those days. There were some that were jealous, I suppose. Don't take it out on me.'

They didn't know I was listening. It was a warm Sunday afternoon, the door was open and I was reading in the back yard. I was only about eleven, I think, but I was terribly upset and angry and cried myself to sleep. Perhaps she was pregnant and had taken some too-drastic measures. She shouldn't have died, anyway. It wasn't fair.

I didn't like my living grandmother too much, but felt really close to my dead one. Typical of me, that was.

Alice stayed just over an hour and when Sarah had let her out and come upstairs and settled down, I put the light on and phoned

Bernard. I knew he wouldn't be in – he's in Turkey or somewhere with Tom – but even leaving a message on his answerphone made me feel closer to him.

He's the only one who's ever really counted. 'But out alack, he was but one hour mine. The region cloud hath masked him from me now.'

Then I put the phone down and cried for quite a long time.

Chapter 11

A sleepless night. All the same, I seem to be in some sort of heavy, drowsy state when Dilys comes to my room with breakfast.

'I don't want to hurry you, love,' she says, 'but it's ten o'clock.'

'Hell! I meant to get you breakfast in bed.'

'I've brought some for you. For both of us. Only coffee and toast.'

She pulls back the curtains and straightens the bedclothes. 'Move up,' she says.

'You seem very spry this morning.'

'Spry. What a horrid word. And now Dilys Hallam, a spry old lady of ninety-two, lets us into the secrets of her boudoir.'

'Did you sleep well?'

'Only for a few hours. Did you?'

'No. To be honest, I started to think about David, and then couldn't stop.'

'Oh God, isn't it time for you to get that pathetic old bore out of your system?'

'Good old Dilys. Sympathetic as ever. Sympathetic and spry.'

We drink our coffee and spread plum jam on our slices of wholemeal toast. It's August Bank Holiday. The morning is grey and there's a light rain pattering on the window, but Alice is home, and on the whole I'm looking forward to the day.

Then something happens. At first I think Dilys is choking, but find that she's trembling, her whole body shaking. 'I'm never going to forgive him,' she says, when she's recovered a little. 'Peter, I mean. I know you think I should, that he was temporarily out of his mind and so on, but I'm not going to. Oh, I'm so incensed at what's happened. I'll never be able to get it out of my mind. And I think I've got a duty to stand up in court and tell people what it was like. At least I'm articulate. At least I won't be frightened of being questioned. Do you remember that swine of a judge who sent some poor seventeen-year-old to prison for twenty-four hours because she couldn't face being cross-examined? Well, I'm going to fight for her. And for all those other girls who're too frightened even to bring charges against the brutes who rape them ... Now you think I'm being histrionic, don't you?'

'No, I don't. I think you're being very brave.'

'Then why did you snatch the tray away?'

'Because there's still coffee in the pot and I didn't want it over your bedspread.'

'That's the trouble with you, Sarah. And I'm being absolutely serious now. There's something hard and self-contained about you. You can never let yourself go, can you? You can never be totally *for* anyone or anything. You're always out on the sidelines worrying about the bedspread. You're on the right side, but you won't commit yourself. You won't even commit yourself to me, will you? Though I need your support – who else have I got? No, you'll be too busy worrying about Peter's state of mind and Alice's part in it, his mother and father's feelings, what David Noel-Smith would think about it all, and all the other things that don't matter a damn.'

She's right. There are few things I can be wholehearted about.

'You're absolutely wrong,' I say. 'I *am* committed to you. And to all those other girls. I'll go into the witness box and say whatever your solicitor tells me to. Honestly.'

She grits her teeth. 'Oh, don't look so bloody martyred. I only want you to tell the truth, for God's sake. I was raped by that brute. He held me down so that I was helpless and rammed his penis into me. Is that something you can be half-hearted about?'

Her anger finishes as suddenly as a meter running out of coins. She slumps down on the pillows and bursts into tears.

For a time, I let her cry, thinking it might do her some good. What can I say? What wise and useless things? 'It'll take you ages to get over it. You mustn't even try to push it out of your mind. It's only through talking about it and facing it that you'll come to terms with it.' Well, I say them all, and then repeat them. And pat her back. And pass her tissues and cold coffee. And promise, over and over again, that I'm on her side.

It's at least half an hour before she pulls herself together and starts to worry about her face.

'I'm too old to cry like this,' she says, getting out of bed and examining herself in the mirror. 'Oh God, I look like my Auntie Lottie. Poor old Auntie Lottie. She had an illegitimate baby and brought disgrace on the family, but now Mervyn, this bastard son of hers, had made a fortune in Canada and, bless her, she has wonderful holidays out there, drinking cherry brandy in his Jacuzzi . . .'

'Is Auntie Lottie the one I met?'

'Of course not. She doesn't get to meet anyone. Except in Canada.'

We get dressed.

'Alice is fine,' I say. 'Worried about you, of course, but otherwise all right. She's been in Rome with the boss of the agency she's going to work for.'

'You remember that Mistwood advert I did last year? "One spray. Safe for the day." That was for them. And so was the vodka one I was up for and didn't get. She'll have to introduce me to him. Is he Graaf or Hamilton?'

'She didn't say. Hamilton, I think. Yes, Charles Hamilton. I wonder if she's up yet? I'll give her a ring. Ask her to come over.'

'Let me phone Hywel first, love. He was very upset about me, poor lamb.'

'So was Ralph. Ralph is still very fond of you, you know.'

'Perhaps.'

Her voice hardens again. 'But I'm certainly not going to start anything with Ralph, if that's what you're planning. I may be at a low ebb, but it's not that low. Anyway, I like Liz too much.'

She takes the tray and goes downstairs.

When I follow her, she's already talking to Hywel, so I go to the kitchen and make some fresh coffee. I think I'm as tired as I've ever been in my life.

I should have had a holiday, a quiet week in Ireland or Scotland. God, I should have managed to get rid of Peter. And he'd have been so much better off if I'd sent him away; certainly not in this mess.

Alice and her men-friends. There have been six or seven that I know about, and probably as many others. Is it my fault that she seems to be pretty nearly promiscuous? When she was growing up, I felt I had little right to lay down moral judgements, and that, in any case, I had little advice to offer. I remember being delighted that she was so outgoing, so different from me. I didn't pause to consider that she was, perhaps, too generous and impulsive. Has she ever loved anyone? 'Do you love Peter?' I used to ask her sometimes. She seemed totally bemused by him. 'He loves me,' she'd say. 'Isn't that enough nonsense to be going on with.' She seems quite as unconcerned about this Charles Hamilton, too. I suppose I should be pleased that she isn't breaking her heart over anyone. All the same, I can't stop worrying about her.

I'm pleased she wasn't pregnant though. That was another of Peter's lies.

Poor Auntie Lottie. And all those others. A whole army of disgraced women who did nothing worse than love a man and have his baby.

'Does she really exist?' I ask Dilys when she comes into the kitchen. 'Auntie Lottie? I've never heard you mention her.'

'Of course she exists. Just about. Dear little mouse of a thing. I'll show you a photo of her. Why are you interested? No-one's

96

been interested in Lottie since 1951 – and that didn't last long. One short summer and it was over for ever. She was a little nursemaid with this doctor's family in the Vale, and the wife's young brother came to stay. That's all we ever knew about it.'

We go into the sitting-room and Dilys gets out the old photograph album; green suede cover with sprays of gold ivy leaves, circa 1935. She says she can smell her grandmother's violet cachous on it, but when I close my eyes and sniff, it only smells old and slightly damp.

The photographs are mostly of weddings and christenings; groups of people outside massive chapels, or more occasionally on seaside outings. The men – grandfathers and uncles – are in the background, eyeing the camera with suspicion; the women, a great tribe of grandmothers, great-aunts and aunts, small and dark-haired in hats, doing their best to smile.

'Here's Uncle Ben who looked after the ponies underground. He didn't talk much, only hup, hup. My Uncle Ifor, the singer. Auntie Mary Ellen used to spend so long polishing his silver cups that one night when she was out at a whist drive, he painted them all green. Here's Auntie Lottie. She's wearing my Auntie Eva's old costume, I recognise that, but I don't recognise the hat, it could be anybody's. And this gormless-looking boy is her son Mervyn. He had asthma as a child, he never went out except to school. Anyway, when he was twenty-one he got some money from the solicitor – Auntie Lottie'd never had anything but seven and six a week – and he went to Canada and made good . . . You didn't have aunties, did you?'

'Nor uncles. Nor cousins. That's probably what made me so hard and self-contained.'

'Who ever said you were hard and self-contained?'

'You did.'

'Oh, I'm not myself, Sarah, you must forgive me. I feel . . . diminished somehow. I've always been an optimist. You know that, always bouncing back, whatever happens. I see parts going to people without half my talent, but I never fret about it for more than half an hour. By the time I get back here I've almost forgotten what I went up to Town for, the disappointment's over. But this has done something terrible to me and I don't think I will get over it. My life has always been based on trust and my trust's been betrayed. I'm probably shallow and frivolous, I'm certainly a show-off, but I've always been outgoing and friendly towards everybody. I've worked at being good company – always ready for a laugh – as much as I've worked at being attractive. I'm not much of a feminist; I've never resented being considered a bit of a sex-object as long as that's not all. Ever since I was fifteen, men have seen me as pretty, good-natured and, yes, sexy, but no-one, before, has ever tried to force me, or even persuade me to do anything I didn't want to do. And now, that bastard! Oh God, it was so humiliating. Do you know, I could hardly bear Ralph near me yesterday. I felt like shuddering when he tried to hold my hand. I've got to see the police doctor again next week and I'm dreading it, dreading being touched.'

'Don't cry again, Dilys. Please. I do realise what you've been through and I'll do everything I can to help you. And, love, you will recover. I promise you. At the moment, you're still in a state of shock. After any injury – an operation or a bad accident – you feel weak and despondent and it sometimes takes months to get back to normal. But you do recover eventually. Do you remember how terribly depressed I was after the abortion? I remember feeling that that was a sort of violation, even though I'd decided on it myself.'

We look hard at each other. Two middle-aged women with the past all around them. 'I was so pretty when I was fifteen,' Dilys says. 'I used to stare at myself in the mirror, hardly able to believe my luck. And now . . .'

'I was sometimes very happy. David seemed to be what I wanted. If only . . .'

The clock strikes twelve, pulling us both up sharp.

'I think I'll go over to call Alice,' I say. 'She'll sleep all day otherwise. Will you come over to have lunch with us? What time is Hywel coming back?'

'Not till tomorrow. Liz is bringing him tomorrow.'

'So, will you come over to us or shall we come here?'

'You decide. My mind's a blank. I know I've got some chops. I don't think I had a meal yesterday.'

'Yes you did. I made you some lunch . . .'

We're having an animated discussion about whether two eggs (scrambled) constitute a meal, when the doorbell rings and Dilys goes to answer it.

I recognise the inspector's voice, though it seems different today: it's lost its cutting edge; he's talking in a normal, civilized way; he could be anyone.

Dilys brings him into the sitting-room.

'I've called to apologise to your friend,' he tells me. 'It's my job to get at the truth and if I was hard on her, I'm sorry.'

'You were pretty hard on me, too.'

'Nonsense.'

'So what's made you change your mind?' Dilys asks. She looked composed again, young and carefree, as she does in her latest advertisement for Sparkle washing-up liquid.

'We've found out that the accused is a dangerous man.'

I feel a sudden chill in my bones. 'My daughter seems to have had a lucky escape,' I say, in a quiet voice.

'She's still in Rome?'

'She came back early this morning.'

'So who finally managed to convince you?' Dilys asks him. 'God knows, I tried hard enough.'

'His father got in touch with us this morning. The accused was allowed bail, partly because of his father's position as parish priest. However, after being in the parental home for some hours, an argument occurred during which he became violent and later escaped. His mother is in hospital having sustained injuries to the head.'

'Where is he now?' I ask. 'Has he been caught?' I can hear my heart beating.

'Not yet. His father failed to notify us last night. He was under the impression – mistaken as it turns out – that his son, the accused, that is to say, would come to his senses and return home.'

'My God, he's got the key to our house. And Alice is alone there.'

Chapter 12

It's about 0200 hours BST when I get back to Foxlawn on the morning of 25 August. I'm very tired, my eyes itchy and sore, but I realise Mum is dying to *Tell all*, so I go in to Dilys's and Mum and I have a heart-to-heart. Tell her about Charlie! Though not everything!

All she wants to talk about is Dilys's *Ordeal*, and I can't really be bothered to think about it. Naturally, I'm furious with Peter, but I've been furious with him for ages, so she isn't really satisfied with my response. I think she's afraid I'm going to accuse Dilys of leading him on, though I'm not. Dilys can't help being a flirt, sixties-style, but this doesn't mean that anyone should take advantage of her. (God, I'd half-kill the bastard that tried it on me. I mean that. Kick to injure. I could and would.)

It's a funny thing, but I find myself seeing Mum in a different way. Somebody that Jack Wells fancies. You see, I've always considered him in rather a favourable light. He's a super badminton player, for instance, and he's got these lovely shoulders and marvellous thighs. And seeing her through his eyes, I realise that she isn't bad-looking for someone her age. Her dress-sense is appalling and she does all the wrong things with make-up, but basically there's nothing much wrong with her face or her body, and these days men are supposed to go for mature women. I think I would be encouraging (and only slightly jealous) if it came to anything. Not that it will.

It's too bad that she's wasted her best years on ol' Spaniel Eyes. Had a tricky moment when she asked me what I'd thought about him. Nearly told her.

Anyway, after she'd insisted on telling me – for the umpteenth time – what a tragic life he'd led, I finally left her and went across the road to our house: No. 5.

By this time it's exactly 0300 hours.

The minute I get in, the phone rings. I take it for granted that it's Mum who's remembered something else she wants to tell me.

'Solly, long number,' I say.

'Alice. Oh Alice.'

It's him, of course. Peter. His voice throbbing with passion or remorse or some other dark emotion.

'Alice. You're back. It's you.'

I have to admit it.

'Alice. I was ringing to ask your mother to give you a message from me.'

'Oh, yes.'

'A last message.'

'A last message,' I say, trying to keep the anger and scorn out of my voice. 'Right, Sir. Let's have it, Sir.'

'Alice. I'm going to kill myself.'

'Oh, for God's sake, Peter, shut up. Don't turn it on. Don't be so bloody melodramatic, for God's sake. Thank God my mother didn't answer the phone or you'd frighten the life out of her. Right, you're going to kill yourself and I've got to talk you out of it, right? How long's it going to take, though, kid, because I've had a lot of broken nights lately and I'm dying on my feet. Where are you? At the vicarage? Look, one piece of advice. If I were you, I should leave there as soon as possible . . .'

I'd never be any fuckin' good as a Samaritan. I simply don't have the patience. For a start, I can't really believe – even though I read the statistics – that anyone can seriously contemplate suicide. God, this is the only life we've got and, however bad today may be, tomorrow could be a dazzler.

102

'Look, Peter,' I say, trying hard to ooze friendliness and understanding. 'However bad things may seem today, tomorrow—'

'Don't give me that crap. Shut up, will you. I'm desperate.'

'I should jolly well think you are,' I say, changing tack. 'You've behaved like a bloody thug. So where are you?'

There's a long pause. 'At that Service Station where we sometimes stop for coffee and doughnuts.'

'All right. I'll be with you in half an hour.'

'I don't want to see you, Alice. No. My mind's made up. My life's over. I don't want to see you again.'

'I don't give a damn, Sonny. You're going to, whether you want to or not. And don't move from where you are. If you do anything stupid, I'll despise you for ever. I mean that.'

'I only wanted to leave a message for you,' he's saying as I slam down the phone.

It's suddenly begun to feel real.

I get my mother's new car from the garage and drive to the motorway, I won't admit how fast.

As I'm driving I'm thinking about holidays in France when I was a kid. It was Peter mentioning stopping for doughnuts that did it – and being so tired. When we were in France, Mum and I used to get up at six every morning so that she could get some driving done while it was still cool and the roads were still clear. We'd leave the campsite without having anything but a fruit juice and we'd drive along these miles of white roads with pine forests on each side, windows open and wonderful pungent smells, and all the way we'd plan what we were going to do that day and especially what we were going to eat. Sometimes I'd fall asleep against Mum's shoulder, waking up to say *artichoux* or *bouillabaisse* from time to time.

When we stopped for breakfast at about nine-thirty, the brioche and coffee was all I wanted in the world. To dip cake in dark coffee and smell it, a shiver of tiredness, and the smell of the grass and the gorse and the sea in the distance. Oh world. 'Earth and the great weather move me. Have carried me away and move my inward parts with joy.' That's by an Inuit woman called Uvavnuk. Something I illustrated in my second year.

While all this is going on in the feeling part of my brain, the planning cells are still actively engaged on the job in hand, i.e., Peter, and have come to this decision: his mind has definitely flipped and I've got to sell him the idea that a spell in a mental hospital will put him right – or as right as he ever was. Art therapy and things. There won't be any question of any sort of legal trial, I shall say to him, not if you put yourself in my hands.

The thing is, I'm convinced that I can persuade Dilys to drop the charge she's brought against him because, in spite of all her silliness, she's really a pretty wonderful person.

I usually try not to think about that night when she came home and found me in bed with her actor boyfriend, Philip Newman. I was around sixteen at the time, and completely besotted by him. He was handsomer and more thrilling than any man I'd ever seen or dreamed about. I'd been watching him in a telly serial set in Crete or some very exotic place, so to me he was Romantic Hero personified. When he followed me to bed – I was at her house baby-sitting, he'd arrived unexpectedly while she was still out – I thought life could hold no greater glory.

When Dilys crept in – I don't know, even now, whether she knew he'd arrived and was looking for him, or whether she was just checking that I was covered up – her fury was absolutely terrifying. Like a storm at sea.

She turned him out of the house there and then – it was long gone midnight – hardly allowing him time to get dressed, certainly not letting him say a word in his own defence (for instance, how I'd been quite openly leching after him for weeks) throwing his shoes and books after him, and shouting so much that she woke Gareth and Tom who went rushing downstairs to enjoy it.

I was sitting up in bed cringing, expecting her to attack me, too, but when she came back to my room, she was very quiet and said she didn't blame me at all. 'You're a child,' she said. 'The fault is all his.'

Honestly, I was ashamed and desperately sorry.

We hugged each other, both sniffing a bit.

I begged her not to tell my mother and I don't think she ever did.

So, you see, I know she's OK under that act she puts on. I'd do quite a lot for her.

(And I think she was very much in love with Philip Newman, too, which makes it worse. Also, they never made it up.)

Anyway, that's why I know Dilys can be counted on to behave charitably to Peter. Or to anyone else, for that matter.

Well, I'm driving like a maniac and get to the Service Station at least ten minutes inside the world record. I look at my watch and wonder just what sort of mad people will be about at this grey hour. Me and Peter Venables, that's who.

I go up to the door of the restaurant, wondering what sort of a pathetic creature I'll find inside.

I see him pressed up against the side of the place, out of the light. 'Alice,' he says.

He seems totally normal.

I've been winding myself up for a massive confrontation, my well-considered arguments all rehearsed and ready, and what I find is this large, unruffled, conventionally dressed, conventionally handsome man who greets me as distantly as though he's my long-lost brother or something. All passion most definitely spent.

'We don't want to hang around here any more,' I say, pitching my voice somewhere between normal aggressive and social worker cheerful. 'Why don't we drive back to Foxlawn? I'm bloody shagged and you look none too perky.'

He follows me to the car, docile as a lamb, harmless as a butterfly.

I unlock the door, get in and lean over to open the other door for him. He comes in without a word of protest. I start the engine. I get back on to the motorway.

I can't seem to think of any topic of conversation, though.

How've you been, would obviously be a bad start, while to tell him about my super time in Rome would probably be worse. Where've you come from? Have you eaten? I can't seem to get started. I'm really horribly tired. I drive in the slow lane at quite a reasonable speed. I think about France again, that stop for breakfast. In an effort to keep awake, I open the window wide.

'I'm going to kill you, Alice,' he says, very quietly.

I wonder if I've heard properly. I wind the window up and turn to face him.

'I'm going to kill you and then kill myself,' he says in the slightly artificial voice of someone making conversation at a party.

I see that he's got a large kitchen knife in his hand, one of these Sabatier things, almost as big as a carving knife.

I decide – perhaps it isn't a decision, more a reflex action – to drive on to the hard shoulder.

'Keep going,' he says, putting the tip of this knife against my ribs.

'You mind this bloody coat,' I say. 'This is haute couture, this is, and if it's marked in any way, brother, I'll never speak to you again. Right?'

'I'm going to kill you,' he says. 'Keep going.'

I'm still not taking him seriously, but I'm seriously beginning to rack my brains about what to do with him. Marvellous ideas keep springing to mind, like making a U-turn and driving back the wrong way, hoping to get arrested, but I'm too bloody tired to carry them out. There's very little traffic about, few people to notice any signals I might try to make. Naturally, there's no sign of a police car.

'How much further do I have to go before you kill me? I haven't got much petrol.'

He leans over to look at the gauge.

There's a sour smell coming from him. Body smells I love; sweat and sex, but this is something different. Fear?

'There's a gallon left even when it shows Empty,' he says.

'You know this car, do you? This model?'

'Keep driving,' he says, when we come to the Shipsley Exit.

I don't think I'm really frightened, but the back of my throat and my tongue are very dry. I'm longing for a drink.

'I'm going to stop, Peter. Look, there's a red light come on. It's dangerous to go any further. I don't intend to ruin my mother's new car, whatever you say. She's worked hard for this car. I'm turning off as soon as I can.'

It's about ten miles to the next exit and this time he doesn't attempt to stop me. I drive through a small village on to a minor road, trying to find my way back home. After a while, I realise I'm going in the wrong direction – am I jetlagged or something? – so I slow down.

'Keep going,' he says, the tip of the knife touching my coat again.

I take a left turn into an even narrower road, still hoping to find my way to home territory, but the road peters out into a track. And I realise what an error I've made. If he really wants to kill me, I've bloody well brought him to the ideal place: a remote country lane where no-one's likely to interrupt him.

The lane winds uphill.

God, there's this nerve in my eyelid beginning to play up, twitching about like mad. It's probably the first sign of complete physical and mental disintegration.

The car comes to a stop. I've been driving since I'm seventeen and it's only the second time I've ever run out of petrol. And this time it's definitely not intentional.

'Get out,' he says.

'Haven't you forgotten that certain little word,' I say through my teeth.

I get out. Slowly. He's right behind me.

The air is chilly. I wonder whether to make a run for it. I'd probably manage to get away, it's a moonlit night, but I'm too bloody tired to summon up the energy.

'Peter,' I say, trying to keep my voice steady. 'Can't you just chuck it in? If I've hurt you, I'm sorry. What more can I say? For God's sake, let's make it up.'

He's so near me, I can feel his breath on the back of my neck.
Suddenly, he plunges his knife into my beautiful new coat and
slashes it all the way down to the hem. The sound of it ripping
is like a rocket going off.

I forget about fear. All I can think of is violation, and I howl
for revenge. I throw my head back and howl like a pack of
wolves and as he looks at me, temporarily abashed, I lunge at
his hand with what might be an uppercut, and the knife flies into
the air, and I fly after it and, oh boy, I get it. And then I face
him, holding the knife in both hands.

'You bloody vandal,' I say. 'I was prepared to be so under
standing. But now all I want is revenge. This coat cost about
million lira.'

'I've left you everything I possess,' he says. 'I've made a will
and left everything to you.'

'A lousy old computer and a stamp collection. Thanks
bunch.'

But I can't go on indefinitely, standing there like the cover of
a paperback called *Wild Love*.

'Turn round,' I say, in a snarling voice. (But now I'm only
acting tough. My anger has gone.)

He's become dispirited, too. Slowly he turns round.

Whatever does he think I'm up to?

What I do is tiptoe some distance away, throw the knife as far
as I can into the thicket – it sounds like a bird flying – and tiptoe
back.

'All right,' I say, after taking a few deep, steadying breaths.
'You can turn round.'

It's a bit like Grandmother's Steps.

'OK, it's gone, and now let's forget about it. OK? This farce
has gone on long enough.'

It doesn't seem like a farce, though, but more like some bloody
Greek tragedy. I want to wake up and find it's all a dream. I
keep on remembering tender little things about Peter, like how
squeamish he is about blood. Did the poor sod really think he
could kill me? The poor sod can't sit through any decent film.

we wanted to go to the cinema we kept on having to see some wretched American comedy.

'What about going back to the car and trying to get some kip,' I say. 'I don't feel like trudging back to the motorway, do you?'

He shrugs his shoulders. Even in the half-light, I can see that he's shut his eyes. Is he praying? Oh God.

We walk back to the car.

'The front seats of this versatile little family saloon are fully reclining,' I say, shaking one of them. 'Down, Bonzo.'

He finds some gadget and helps me push them back as far as they'll go. '*Bene, Bene,*' I say. '*Multo perfecto.*' Exhausted as I am, I'm still doing my good-old-Alice act.

I take off my ruined coat, then lie back in the driver's seat, tucking it round me.

'Come on,' I say. 'Come on in and try and make yourself comfortable. There's nothing else you can do, Peter. If I thought you had a chance out there, I'd tell you to go. But you haven't, love.'

After a while, he gets in and lies back on the other seat, his hands behind his head.

'I want to die, Alice,' he says.

Oh Christ Almighty.

Chapter 13

Alice isn't anywhere in the house. Her bed hasn't been slept in. Her canvas bag is still in the hall unopened.

'Where is she?' I ask Dilys and the inspector who have followed me in. 'She wouldn't have gone out without leaving a note for me. Where is she?'

Dilys and I go from room to room looking for signs of her. We find none.

She hasn't been anywhere. She hasn't even had a cup of coffee. 'This is the way I leave things,' I say, 'not the way she does. If she'd had a coffee, the kitchen would look . . . different. If she'd sat in the sitting-room for even five minutes, well it would look . . .'

'Different,' Dilys tells the inspector. 'Cushions and magazines and CDs on the floor. You know what they're like. It only takes them five minutes.'

'She must have had a phone call as soon as she got in,' I say. 'That's why her bag is still in the hall.'

'Who'd phone her at three a.m.?' the inspector asks. 'Who'd know she was home?'

'Peter would be the only one about at three a.m.' Dilys says. 'He must have phoned asking her to meet him somewhere.' She starts to shiver again.

I press caller-return only to find that Ralph had phoned at ten-thirty, wanting news of Dilys I suppose, so that was no help.

'Hold on,' the inspector says. 'We mustn't jump to conclusions. She wouldn't have gone out to meet someone she knows to be a rapist.'

'She didn't know it,' Dilys says. 'Even you didn't believe it until you had that phone call from his father. She probably thought he was practically blameless. Just as you did.'

'Let's be calm,' the inspector says, giving her a cool sideways look.

He ushers us back to the sitting-room and gets us to sit down. 'I've got to speak to the chief,' he says. 'It will only take two minutes.'

He closes the door. We can't hear what he's saying, though we do our best. 'The police will be able to trace that three a.m. call,' Dilys says. 'They're thick but they're not stupid.'

'She's such an idiot, so impulsive. She'd do anything for anyone. She'd go anywhere.'

The room is full of a hard white light.

Suddenly my heart lifts. 'Dilys! You know I got Jack Wells to fetch her from Heathrow last night? What if she just decided to spend the night with him? I know he made a pass at her. She more or less told me so. She might have been feeling lonely and—'

'No,' Dilys says, 'it doesn't ring true.'

The inspector comes back. (I've almost started liking him by this time.) 'I've had an idea,' I say. 'She may have gone to see a colleague of mine who lives in Albert Terrace.'

'At three in the morning?'

'He was the one who met her at the airport, because I had to stay with my friend. And she told me he'd been ... well ... friendly towards her. And his wife's left him and ... well ... she may have ... well ...'

'She wouldn't have,' Dilys says. 'Alice and Jack Wells. Don't make me laugh.'

'Alice and Peter Venables. That seems quite as unlikely to me.'

'Why not ring the gentleman in question?' the inspector says

'Or would you like me to call on him?'

'Of course not,' I say quickly. 'He's a perfectly respectable man. She's twenty-two, you know, not fifteen. If anyone's to blame, she is.'

I ring Jack's number. There's no reply.

'Don't waste any more time,' Dilys says angrily. 'Face facts. She went out to meet that thug and no-one's doing anything about it.'

'Does she drive?' the inspector asks. 'Does she have a car?'

'She drives mine.'

'Is your garage locked? I'd better check whether she's taken it.'

I give him the key and Dilys and I stand in the porch waiting for him to come back. I'm finding it difficult to swallow.

'Yes, it's gone,' he says. 'And since we can't dismiss the possibility that she went out to meet him, we'll need to circulate the description of the car.'

I give him the details he wants, colour, make and registration number. I also give him a recent photograph of Alice.

'He must have rung her,' Dilys says. 'He must have got stuck somewhere and phoned asking her to pick him up.'

'But he didn't even know she was home,' I say. 'He wouldn't have phoned at three in the morning.'

The police inspector says nothing, just looks at us both, pockets Alice's photograph and leaves.

Every other car on the road is a red Metro,' Dilys says. 'They'll never be able to trace it.'

'We may have a long time to wait, so we must do our best to keep calm,' I say, feeling more and more agitated by the minute.

Pictures of Alice flash through my mind; at three or four, hurling herself from the swing in the park to cling to whatever down-at-heel mongrel that had happened to come by; at about six, and in trouble with someone. 'Were you responsible for . . .?' A toss of the head. 'It's possible.' In fights, often with a much bigger child, the way she'd shake away her tears, swear and spit, but never give in. How old was she when we had to go to the casualty department of the hospital to have the gash in her knee stitched? 'It's nothing,' she kept saying, anxious that I shouldn't make too many inquiries about whose bike she'd been riding. 'It's nothing.' I still remember her clenched face.

I should be used to worrying about her. The very first time she went to a rock concert in Wembley, the coach she was in broke down on the motorway and she wasn't back till three. 'It wasn't my fault,' she was saying, as I shouted at her. 'How could I let you know when we were miles from a phone box? Why are you so unreasonable?'

Because I'd been afraid I'd never see her again, that's why . . .

'I'm going to ring Ralph,' Dilys says. 'He's a fucking old bore, but he may know if there's anything else we can do.'

She dials his number, but there's no reply there, either.

'Damn, I remember now. He's got a day off today. He was going to take Hywel to the Safari Park. What a day for it.'

We both look out of the window. It's a typical Bank Holiday afternoon, wet and blustery, the sky which was sailor-boy-blue an hour ago is now grey as pewter, the light pale-mauve.

'There's nothing we can do,' I say. 'That's what makes it so difficult. The only way I can comfort myself is by remembering all the other times I've worried myself sick and she's been all right. She's always boasting about how she can look after herself. She's certainly strong. If she did go out to meet Peter, wouldn't she be a match for him? She'd be on her guard, after all, and she's very quick-witted and agile.'

In spite of my brave words the nerves of my stomach are quivering like telegraph wires.

The phone goes and I rush to answer it.

'Sarah, this is David.'

David! I can hardly believe it. I take a deep breath. He hasn't phoned me for almost a year. Not since—

'David. How are you?'

I haven't seen him since the end of term, haven't had a privat conversation with him for almost a year. I can't think what to say.

'I'd like to see you, Sarah. Would this afternoon be a convenient time?'

He wants to see me. My heart is thumping painfully against my ribs. My throat is dry.

'Not this afternoon, David. I'm afraid I'm ... engaged this afternoon.'

Engaged in waiting. For the police to catch a rapist and bring home my daughter.

'I see.' A short pause. 'May I ring up again to suggest another time?'

'Yes, please do. Yes. Another time. Yes. Yes, that would be .. fine.'

He puts the phone down. I hear the click drowning in my head, echoing, until at last it sounds like a door slamming in the distance. I can't seem to move. Why couldn't I have explained to him how it is with me? Why couldn't I have explained about Alice? He was always interested in Alice, fond of her. Why am I such an idiot where he's concerned, always paralysed by nerves?

I turn to Dilys. 'That was David,' I tell her.

'I know it was David, you stupid goop. You're white as a sheet and your voice has gone all humble again. Why didn't you tell him to get stuffed? Listen, I've thought of something I can do. I can go home to get that bottle of gin Ralph brought me.'

You never try to understand how I feel about David,' I say later when she's back and we're sitting in front of the electric fire with a couple of drinks.

'I understand it perfectly. I felt exactly the same about our Head Boy when I was sixteen.'

'You're so unfair. It's not at all that sort of adolescent love. I don't worship the ground he walks on, and all that rubbish. I recognise that he has faults, that he's weak, always tormented by things in the past, which a stronger man would be able to forget. It doesn't make any difference. I love him.'

115

'You love him, warts and all. Fifty-eight years old, thin on top and feeble-minded.'

'Oh shut up. There's such a thing as a love which needs no justification. That's what I mean.'

'Very godly, I must say. Try being a bit more human. Try loving people because they're lovable. Because they love you. Because they need you. Because you could be happy together. Instead of unhappy.'

'I was happy with David.'

'Like hell, you were. You were tormented by guilt. You suffered as much about his wife as he did.'

'I lived for those Wednesday evenings when he came here. The days in between were meaningful and happy because they led to that evening.'

'You weren't happy. God, when he came here, all he could do was drink tea and moan.'

'That was at the end. When Laura was dying.'

'She was dying all along. I wish you'd never met him.'

'So do not I.'

'So do not I?'

'Desdemona.'

'Desdemona. Listen. I've played Desdemona. And I got more passion out of it on the stage in front of three hundred people than you did on all your precious Wednesday evenings.'

'The trouble with you is that your mind can only encompass physical love. There's love, you know, as well as making love. Sex isn't everything. Anyway, if you think we didn't make love you're quite mistaken.'

I can hardly continue, remembering the way he'd raise himself up on an elbow to look at me. 'I'll think of this,' he used to say. 'This is what I'll think about all week,' he used to say. His heart in his eyes . . . Or so I thought. I musn't think of it. I've trained myself not to think of it.

'God, I'm not trying to deny that you made love. God, I used to have Alice over on all those Wednesdays, if you remember to give him every encouragement. Poor sod couldn't get started

116

f she was around. So I had to go out every Wednesday evening, whether I wanted to or not, so that Alice could be in our house baby-sitting.'

'You were very good to me, Dilys.'

'Of course I was. Not everyone would have put up with a sexy seventeen-year-old creating havoc in their lover's breast.'

'What lover was that?'

'Philip. Philip Newman. You speak as though I've had dozens.'

'Philip Newman. You were better off without him. You never knew when he'd turn up. If at all.'

'He was always busy. He was a very successful actor. Still is.'

I shrug my shoulders. I don't mean anything by it because I've never seen him act. He was certainly handsome, certainly very flamboyant, perhaps he could mouth lines, too, as well as anyone.

But Dilys is dabbing her eyes again. I've never known her as touchy.

'I didn't like Philip Newman because he wasn't careful enough of you,' I say. 'He's probably a very good actor.'

She continues to sniff. 'He used to get up really early on a Thursday morning, hoping for a glimpse of Alice in her bra and pants. God, what we put up with.'

' "It does not touch the love still kept for Her," ' I begin to say, but can't be bothered to continue. Alice is back in my mind. Not that she's ever really left it.

'Do you think I should have told David about Alice being missing?' I ask Dilys.

'No,' she says wearily. 'What could he do? One of God's weaklings.'

'Why do you think he wants to see me? I mean, after so long?'

'He's probably getting married again. Wants you to be the first to know. Feels he owes you that much.'

'Dilys, why are you being so spiteful?'

'I'm trying to be realistic. Prepare yourself for the worst and you won't be disappointed. I've always been a bloody optimist and look where it's got me. If I'd been on my guard, always thinking the worst of everyone, I wouldn't have let Peter near me, would I? And I wouldn't be in this state now.'

'You're going to be all right,' I say. 'Come on, you're already much better than you were yesterday.'

'I'm not. I'm not. I'm a cripple, mentally and physically. I'll never be able to face sex with anyone ever again.'

'Darling, don't be absurd. I thought I'd never have the courage to drive again after that lorry crashed into me last year, but you insisted I drove your car the very next day and I got over it in no time.'

'Meaning I've got to find myself a lover within the next few hours. Is that why you got Ralph over yesterday? Thank you for nothing.'

The doorbell rings and we both jump; Dilys is as nervous as I am. After a moment's hesitation, we go to the door together.

It's Jack Wells.

I'm so pleased to see him. 'Oh Jack, do come in. I've been trying to get you on the phone. Was Alice with you last night? After you'd brought her back, I mean.'

'No, she wasn't. Certainly not. I've had a bloody policeman at the house asking the same thing. What the hell's it all about?'

'She's missing, Jack. And so is Peter. I told you about Peter being given bail and going back to London with his mother. Well, there was a disagreement and he left there late last night. And we're afraid he must have persuaded Alice to go somewhere to meet him.'

'Oh, no!' Jack says. 'She wouldn't have gone, surely?'

'She's taken Sarah's car,' Dilys says. 'Where else would she have gone? Her bed hasn't been slept in.'

'Is there anything we can do?' I ask him. 'Can you think of anything? It's nerve-racking to be sitting here doing nothing.'

'We ought to have some lunch,' Dilys says. 'I should have thought of that. We'll start to feel faint if we don't eat. Jack, can you stay for a sandwich? Where are the kids?'

'I left them at the stables. I'm picking them up tomorrow

Look, why don't I go to the Crown to get us some ham rolls?'

'It's too late,' Dilys says. 'By the time you get there it'll be two-thirty. No, I'll make some sandwiches. And what about some soup first? It's cold enough.'

She makes me stay in the sitting-room as though I'm an invalid – or in mourning – with Jack in attendance.

'She wanted you to go back to Italy with her,' Jack says. 'She said you'd love it in Rome. Keats and that.'

Oh Jack, please don't talk as though she's dead, I'm thinking. I don't say anything though, just try to smile.

'She's great, isn't she,' he says then. 'Dilys, I mean. And there was I thinking she was, well, a very frivolous sort of person. Never mind, I'm a lousy judge of character. Fancy that poor sod turning out to be a rapist, for God's sake. What's gone wrong with the world?'

I can't think of anything to say, but it doesn't seem to matter. He's soon in full flow.

'What we must do,' he says, 'is try to put ourselves in his place. He phoned here last night expecting to speak to you. Now, where was he? He'd be on his way back here. Somehow I imagine him in an all-night café on the outskirts of Birmingham. Or would he have got nearer by . . . what time was it Alice left you?'

'About three. Three a.m.'

'Yes. Three a.m. He's in a terrible state after a quarrel with his parents.'

'After a fight with his parents. His mother's in hospital, badly injured.'

'Good God. Three a.m. He's in a terrible state; shock and anger and guilt. He sees a phone box. He's oblivious of the time. All he can think of is that he wants to make contact with Alice. It's his lifeline. He can hardly dial the number. At last he gets through. And it's Alice who answers him. He tells her he's in trouble. Will she help him. Will she help him . . . to do what? What in God's name would he say, to make that girl agree to go out at that hour? Oh Christ, why didn't she phone me to ask me to go with her? She must have realised she was intent on some-

119

thing extremely foolhardy. What could he have said to her? Alice, he said, you must help me.'

I can hardly bear to listen to him rambling on. It sounds like one of his lessons. Alice has disappeared, so how can knowing her exact state of mind help us?

Dilys brings in a tray with three bowls of bright red soup (from a tin), a pepper mill, some grated cheese and some hot croutons (from a packet).

'What a superb meal,' Jack says. 'Dilys, you're a marvel. And I've always thought of you as just . . .'

'Start eating,' she says, 'and keep your dirty thoughts to yourself.'

We eat.

'Good Lord, this is superb,' I keep saying, turning my eyes to the ceiling.

'He must have told her either a) that he'd been badly hurt and needed urgent help or b) that he was going to kill himself if she didn't come to meet him,' Jack continues, as soon as he's finished eating. 'And I favour b) because if a) she'd have insisted on calling an ambulance. OK, he's on the phone. Alice, he says, I'm ringing to say goodbye. I'm in trouble and I'm going to kill myself.'

Dilys joins in. 'For God's sake, Peter, things aren't that bad.'

'I'm at the end of my tether. I can't live through this . . . this disgrace.'

'Don't say that, Peter. Let me come to you. Let me talk to you. Where are you?'

'I'm at the kiosk outside The Little Chef on Windsor Avenue. I'm going to lie down behind one of the lorries in the car-park. The driver won't see me till it's too late.'

'Don't do that, Peter. Stay in the kiosk till I come. I beg you. I'll be with you in forty minutes. Wait for me, Peter. Wait. I beg you.'

'God, you're a superb actor,' Jack says. 'Absolutely great.'

'You're both pretty good,' I say, 'but how does it help? How does dramatising it help?'

'Do you think it sound feasible though?' Jack asks.

'Yes,' Dilys says. 'That's just what happened. It must be. He blackmailed her into going out.'

'I suppose so,' I say. 'If he was threatening to commit suicide, suppose she'd have had to go to him ... But what happened when she got there, that's what I want to know?'

We sit back desolately, lost in our own thoughts.

Chapter 14

I wonder if Sarah blames me for what's happened? If I'd managed to be sweet and understanding towards Peter in the pub, things might have turned out differently. I keep assuring her that Alice is perfectly safe, and I really believe it – she's much bigger and stronger than I am, and much younger – but I know she can't stop worrying.

Perhaps it's just as well that David phoned her this afternoon, so that she's at least got something else on her mind.

For years she dreamed of marrying David; at least, I suppose she did. They might even have been happy together because Sarah is a sweet, selfless person who doesn't expect much out of life. And David isn't much. In fact he's one of the greyest men I've ever met, a headmaster to the core, but probably kind. All right, he's kind and conscientious and hard-working; admirable in every way . . . And grey as a cloud.

I know there are happy marriages, marriages where people continue to find more pleasure in each other than frustration, but they must be pretty rare. Many couples stay together because it's less trouble and less messy than separating. I wish I'd stayed with Bernard, made a determined effort to change myself instead of him . . . But it's too late now.

I don't suppose I'd have been happy without all the emotion; the mystery and fear. Bernard was never easy, never a docile, manageable husband, not even at the beginning. Even at the beginning, I could never make arrangements for both of us, could only say that I'd come to lunch or dinner or to see a film and that he might be free. I was never sure of him. He worked hard at different locations and when he'd finished there was often a party or some other function he had to go to, or someone he simply had to see.

At other times when he turned down invitations and came straight home, he liked those to be special occasions too, but I couldn't ever let them pass without trying to air my grievances. 'Wasn't there anything worth going to tonight?' I'd ask, trying to sound flippant and not too unhappy, 'Wasn't there anyone worth seeing?'

'You're always worth seeing, baby.'

'Oh, I'm just your wife, just the woman you married because you got her pregnant.'

'You don't have to be just a wife! You seem to like putting yourself down. You're an actress and a pretty good actress. When I saw your Nora, I felt the hairs rising on the back of my neck. You can be Dilys Wynne, if you want to, most promising newcomer 1976.'

'What difference would that make?'

'Try it. You can be whoever you choose. You could be a prostitute if that would make you happier. I could ring up from the Station and ask if you were free.'

'Don't be silly.'

'It's not silly. I think you'd like it. I know I'd like it. You could come downstairs to let me in in that red satin wrap and do a little striptease as you took me upstairs.'

'Don't be silly.'

'Is this silly?'

'No, this is a normal married couple undressing each other before making love.'

'And it's lovely. But if you wanted to wear a G-string and a cut-away bra and put lipstick on your nipples and do a little slow dance for me first, that might make it even more lovely. I think you might find it more lovely as well, particularly if you pretended I was someone you'd just picked up, someone who excited you so much that you wanted to give him the best night of his life.'

'Oh stop it. Come to bed. Put the light off. I want to make love.'

'Ask for it then. Show me your body . . . Properly. I want to see all of it.'

'I won't. I've just had a baby. I'm still half a stone overweight. You just want to embarrass me.'

'How can you think that? You're beautiful. If you've put on weight, it suits you. Your breasts are lovely, not large, but large enough to swing about a bit, and your nipples are big and they get hard as soon as I touch them and you've got lovely dark circles around them that weren't there before. If I was seeing you for the first time, I couldn't wait to get my hands on you, all over you too. You're a little cracker, you are. No, I'm not going to put the light off. Turn round for me. Slowly. Now feel my cock. Feel it jumping for you. Tomorrow I'll get you some tarty black underwear and some gold shoes with five-inch heels. Because you love it, don't you? I should have known you'd love a bit of this. And a bit of this. And a bit of this.'

Oh, I suppose I did love it, but I was always embarrassed too. It seemed demeaning to dress up like a whore and then undress again and do all the strange things he wanted me to. 'Now lie face downwards on the bed as though you're totally exhausted. As though your last client has really worn you out. As though you can hardly bear me to touch you. Oh, I'll have to be so gentle with you tonight. I'll get some warm soapy water and give you a gentle little sponge-bath, shall I? Does this feel good? I love washing you here. Does it soothe you? Really?'

Wasn't it demeaning to have one's lawful wedded husband getting worked up because he was imagining me with somebody else, some great muscular brute who'd hurt me and worn me out? I suppose it was, but it was certainly exciting. All our fantasies were exciting. Sometimes he phoned me with such peculiar suggestions that I laughed out loud to hear them, but as soon as

I put the phone down, they seemed to throb inside me, torturing me until he came home.

Sometimes he'd ring up saying he loved me and lusted after me. Sometimes he said all he wanted was to lick me under the chin, that's all. Would I let him lick me under the chin? Of course I would. And my thin, thin shoulder blades? Yes? Right, because that was all he wanted, all he wanted. I was his holy shrine and all he wanted was to kneel before me and worship me with his tongue.

But these moods could never be guaranteed to last. By the time he got home he might want some very different things – or nothing. But I agreed and wanted to do every strange and bizarre thing he suggested; I was under his spell, I know that.

Occasionally I wished we were a more normal couple, but usually concluded that neither I nor anyone else really knew what normal was. I suppose I could have lived quite happily with a life of fantasy.

It was the thought that he might be having fantasies with other women that outraged me. And the fact that he'd never lie about them to make me happier.

'I know it's shameful of me but, darling, you're not suffering from it are you? Do I ever reject you? When you want me? Has there ever been one single occasion? Wouldn't it be fairer to wait till that happens before attacking me? I'd love you to come to Edinburgh/Madrid/Tahiti with me, but I know and you know that you wouldn't leave the boys ... Of course you could if you wanted to. You could leave them with your parents or even with my parents, but you won't. Because you're a little Welsh Puritan and you like to suffer, that's the reason. But you mustn't blame me for it. I don't like suffering. It bores me. Yes, perhaps I will have a little dalliance while I'm away, but it will be completely unimportant, I promise you, and it won't make the slightest bit of difference to you and me. Because I love you, that's why. No, not because you're my wife and the mother of my sons. Because you're a little Welsh Puritan and a dainty little tart as well.'

I wasn't up to dealing with someone like Bernard. I was used to the macho types who went out drinking with their mates every night, but were never unfaithful. They might be too tired after the rugby practice, incapacitated after the seven or eight pints in the club afterwards, to have sex even with their wives, but at least they didn't screw anyone else.

For me, fidelity was completely and terribly necessary.

I wonder if any couple has really solved the jealousy problem. Is having an open relationship any sort of answer? I can't see that it would have made any difference to me; for me other men didn't exist. I didn't want freedom, I only wanted Bernard. I suppose some people are more successful at hiding their hurt and resentment, so that they're able to carry on, pretending that everything's OK. I tried, God knows.

When he was away for two or three weeks, I'd keep myself busy; planning little dinner parties for friends and outings with the children, pushing the thoughts of his inevitable 'dalliance' to the back of my mind, being cheerful whenever he phoned, being loving and welcoming at the station when I met him.

A carefully chosen dinner, an early night and beautifully prolonged sex, sweet and close, and a climax which was like two halves being sucked back together after long absence. And then the aftermath, the warmth and sweat, the heavy limbs, the slack breathing. A few minutes' deep peace. 'I love you.' 'I love you.'

'Then why the fuck do you need anyone else?' I'm suddenly crying out, digging my nails into his shoulder and sobbing. 'Why? Why?'

And Bernard, prepared to be tolerant for a few minutes, finally wrenching himself away from me, 'I can't take any more of this,' and stamping downstairs, putting on a record, turning up the volume, noisily making up a bed on the sofa.

While I'm trying to get to grips with the situation, trying to bear it, trying to live through it when all I feel is the walls moving together till I'm almost suffocating in the thick darkness, the fibres of my heart straining, the pain agonising, the twanging in my head unbearable. And then one coherent thought rising through the pain: 'I must leave him, I must leave him.' And falling asleep with that thought. And waking for the children in a few hours with it still in my mind. 'I must leave him.'

If only I'd been a different type. If only I'd loved him less, I suppose I could have enjoyed his exuberance and tolerated his infidelity. But I was idealistic and unsophisticated and finally became too hurt and bewildered to take any more. And for a time I managed to convince myself that I was happier without him.

And almost as soon as I'd insisted on a divorce, I met Ralph, and because he was the complete opposite of Bernard in every way I managed to convince myself that he was what I needed, or what I deserved. (We met in a supermarket on one of those hopeless, rainy days when I shouldn't have bothered to go out, shouldn't have bothered to get up. He seemed very large and capable and kind. He was all those things, but a lot of other things as well, such as humourless, opinionated, unimaginative and despotic.)

Thank God I had the courage to admit my mistake before too long. We only lived together for just over three years, but even that seemed endless.

And since he's left I've had two or three affairs, well, three in fact, all quite uplifting in their way but all of them with built-in obsolescence. And I didn't even want any of them to last, wasn't really committed to any of them.

Philip Newman, my last living-in lover, was nearly ten years younger than me which was very fashionable at that time. He was an actor, very good-looking and successful and he got on well with the boys. (Ralph doted on Hywel, but was very strict with Gareth and Tom, another thing which maddened me; they were my children, mine and Bernard's, and nothing to do with him. But the problem with Philip was that he took himself too damned seriously. He had a good body, yes, but he was for ever exercising it; he had a set of weights and various little contraptions for shaping his thighs and his calves and tightening his buttocks and he really expected me to enjoy watching him working out. I thought it was ludicrous. It was like having to pander to another child.

He wasn't very good at sex either, in spite of his muscles, because he was much more interested in his body than in mine. And he always wanted to bath afterwards which I found insulting. He never made me laugh.

The crunch came when he started being interested in Alice. She was about sixteen or seventeen at the time and naturally overwhelmed when this great-looking guy she'd often seen in romantic leads on the telly started to appear before her in little boyish shorts and shirt open to the navel to reveal shiny brown skin and the mat of hair on his manly chest. (I don't think he actually wore a gold medallion, but you always felt he might.)

I can't believe that he lusted after Alice in any red-blooded way – that would have made it more excusable – I think the fact was that she, so newly-made and doting, assuaged his vanity, made him feel a star.

I went completely beserk when I found them in bed together. I'd realised it was in both their minds and I'd been careful not to give them the opportunity, but that evening I wasn't careful enough.

Well, I screamed abuse and threw things at him, as though he'd broken my heart, but of course it was Bernard I was punishing, it was bloody Bernard I wanted to maim and debase. So I thumped poor Philip Newman and pulled his hair and threw his clothes at him and all his beautiful Italian shoes and his vast array of toiletries and turned him out of the house there and then. Gareth and Tom were sitting on the stairs by this time looking very awed or very nervous, I wasn't sure which, and I shouted 'Bed!' at them without offering any explanation and they scurried off.

I can't remember where Alice was by this time or what I said to her. I know I felt I'd been negligent, but perhaps she'd enjoyed it. She'd had a couple of affairs before this; I remember I was always passing her articles from the *Guardian*'s Woman's Page and little packets of condoms in case Sarah was too embarrassed.

I'd tried having heart-to-heart chats with her too, but we always ended up giggling.

I wonder what she'll do now. She's growing into a lovely girl – warm and intelligent. When she's able to stop posturing and be herself, she'll be someone special; she's self-assured, unconventional, challenging, all the things I wanted to be and failed. What will she do when she's managed to extricate herself from Peter and this mess he's got her into? All sorts of exciting things; it's all in front of her.

There'd be a fair amount in front of Sarah too if she could open her eyes and notice the way Jack Wells looks at her. He's twice the man David Noel-Smith is or ever was, but she'd need some colossal shock to make her realise it. There's simply no point in my saying anything. I've already said too much. And why should she think I know best? The way I've run my life can't instil much faith into anyone.

I know I've become bitter and intolerant, I feel insecure and unfulfilled, and I accept that my acerbity was too much for Peter; yes, I accept part of the blame for what happened. Sarah was always warm and sympathetic towards him, but it wasn't working, he was getting worse rather than better. I felt I needed to be harsh, needed to make him face up to the fact that Alice had left him and wouldn't be coming back. Yes, I accept that I over-did it, perhaps I was even cruel. I admit I've never said such hard-hitting things to anyone else. But all the same, there was no excuse, no possible bloody excuse for what he did. I could forgive him if he'd shaken me or hit me or knocked me about. But he rammed his penis into me and raped me and I'll never get over that, I'll never forgive him for that. It wasn't the pain or the humiliation, but the fact that he destroyed something, destroyed everything. I still feel a tight band of iron around my heart, a dark horror in my head.

All I can do now is try to make another new start, to begin working again. I'll buy a copy of *Contacts* tomorrow and start writing letters. I'll have to have some new photographs too.

Chapter 15

The day is getting steadily worse, more and more unbearable. By four o'clock I'm feeling really desperate.

I feel sure that Alice is in some real danger, but whenever I say so, Dilys only pours me another drink.

'All right, perhaps she is in danger,' she says, 'but listen, that kid has thrived on danger all her life. Do you remember how she went for those louts who were threatening Hywel on Bonfire Night last year? Three or four of them and they just turned tail and ran. Do you remember how she tackled the burglar at Susan Elliot's? When you and I were cowering in the garden? Hasn't she always enjoyed confrontation? Listen to me, Sarah, Alice is OK, she's safe and well and getting things sorted out.'

'Do you know the poem about that little Isabel?' Jack asks us. 'I was reading it to Stevie the other night and it made me think of Alice:

> Ho ho, Isabel, the old witch crowed,
> I'll turn you into an ugly toad!
> Isabel, Isabel, didn't worry,
> Isabel didn't scream or scurry,
> She showed no rage and she showed no rancour,
> She turned the witch into milk and drank her.'

I'm astonished to hear Jack reciting a poem, even an Ogden

Nash. He pretends to be so scathing about literary people. Has he been teasing me for the whole time – about ten years – that we've been teaching in the same school. Why? To mock my too-intense enthusiasms, I suppose, my high seriousness. I think perhaps most of the members of staff laugh at me behind my back.

The truth is that I simply don't find it easy to make friends, to get accepted in any circle. I've always noticed that the atmosphere of the common-room changes when I go in. Suddenly there isn't so much noise and laughter, people seem to become aware of their next lesson, of various commitments, various problems. It's not that I've ever encountered definite hostility either at school or anywhere else. It's less than that. Just a sense of distance, I suppose. I've never quite understood it.

I've always assumed that it's something to do with the way I was brought up; the lack of brothers and sisters and the hurly-burly of ordinary family life.

Today, I'm not so sure. Perhaps I've always been too ready to blame my parents for all my weaknesses. Certainly, we never became a close family unit. In my early memories, I always seem to be with the au pair. It was she who took me to and from school, to my Saturday dancing class and for a walk on a Saturday afternoon, and I think I was always resentful.

My parents had had ten years of marriage before I was born; they'd obviously planned to remain childless. I must have been a shocking inconvenience to them. But what can I accuse them of except being too wrapped up in each other? They were always very considerate towards me.

When Geoff got drowned, they put themselves out to help me in every way. Yes, they were relieved when I decided to come back here to attempt to lead my own life, but they'd have been fully prepared to have me stay with them if that had been my choice.

When I decided to go to University, they were very surprised, but couldn't have been more supportive, getting me a car for the travelling I had to do and paying in full for the Nanny I had to have for Alice. I should be thanking my stars.

Why am I always so grudging towards them? They hadn't wanted me, but they always did their best to love me and, occasionally, I think, very nearly succeeded.

They live, now, in a sheltered complex for the elderly – sorry, senior citizens – near Folkestone and seem relatively contented, fussing about each other as they always have.

They're pleased to see me when I visit them, but never put out when I have to postpone a trip, or because I don't go more often. My mother is still elegant and beautifully dressed. She seems much younger than her age though her hands have become too arthritic for piano-playing or even embroidery. She doesn't go out much – my father does their shopping – she rests in the afternoon, reads thrillers by the dozen and watches television as long as it's not 'disturbing' (people killing each other doesn't upset her, but people taking their clothes off and going to bed together is certainly 'disturbing').

My father is slightly stooped, a little deaf, more than a little intolerant towards black youth, bikers, hippies, lefties and most of the two million unemployed. So. They're the products of their upbringing, their background, their parents.

Perhaps I shall go to see them next week. It's time, I tell myself, for me to stand – or fall – without trying to blame them for all my shortcomings.

And as I'm making that resolve, I'm dredging something else up. A little painting I once did for my mother's birthday when I was thirteen or so. I remember it vividly – dark pine trees against a pink sunset – it took me hours of effort. I can't actually remember presenting it to her. What I remember is coming across it some time later, not framed and treasured as I'd hoped, but discarded with a pile of old magazines.

Well, she was always absent-minded. She probably thought it was something she'd acquired in a Church sale. The fact that I've harboured that slight for almost thirty years probably says more about me than about her, something about being hard and intolerant.

I turn to Jack, trying to direct my unease at him. 'I don't know why you pretend to be such a Philistine,' I say, my voice unsteady. 'I simply don't understand why you always find it necessary to tease me.'

To my surprise, he looks me in the eye and says, 'It's because you put on such a superior act, that's why. You always go out of your way to avoid any real contact with any of us.'

That's straight enough.

'You never join in,' he continues. 'Whatever's going on, whatever anyone tries to arrange. You never come to the pub on a Friday evening, for instance. Almost everyone else tries to turn up occasionally, for a drink or a game of skittles.'

'I can't play skittles. I don't like crowds of people in pubs.'

'Neither do I, as a matter of fact. Only it's a way of getting to know people, a way of meeting colleagues on an equal footing, a way of showing you're ready to be friendly. You always say, "I don't think I can manage it. There's a possibility that . . ." You like to keep your distance. You think . . .'

'Oh, what bloody nonsense,' Dilys says.

I hear them arguing about me, but it seems a long way off.

I'm lucky that Dilys is such a friendly, self-confident person, that she never noticed any barrier I may have put up. She moved here when Alice was seven years old and I was doing my post-graduate teacher training year at Oxford. The very capable Nanny I'd had for three years had left to get married and I'd got a pretty poor replacement, not bad enough to get rid of – she did her best in her own way – but staid and unimaginative, and every Sunday evening I was more and more worried about leaving Alice with her.

One Friday when I got home, Alice couldn't wait to tell me her news. 'I've got a new friend,' she said. 'She's called Dilys and she's moved into Number Eight and I go to play with her after school and once I had my tea there.'

Wonderful, I thought. There were very few young children in Foxlawn then. Most of the houses – four-bedroomed, neo-Georgian – were owned by older people whose children were either teenagers or had already left home. I decided that I'd call at No. 8 and have Dilys over.

'How old is she?' I asked.

'I don't know, but she's very nice. I'm allowed to watch her television whenever I want.'

I had a moment's unease. At that time I was being a conscientious mummy, limiting her viewing to Blue Peter and Jackanory.

As I put her to bed, I became even less enthusiastic about her new friend. She'd suddenly acquired a rich new vocabulary. 'Mrs Tiggywinkle? Oh no, Mrs Tiggywinkle's a smelly old poo ... Oh God, Mummy, isn't this dead boring. Oh God.'

I managed to ignore her frequent interruptions, but all the same, bedtime that night was rather fraught.

That weekend, like most at that time, was planned to the minute. At half past ten, after I'd finished a large pile of ironing, Alice and I went to Sainsbury's where she pushed the trolley and I got food for the next week. This was followed by an hour in the park; swings and ducks, or in the library if the weather was impossible, followed by our Saturday lunch of cream cheese, salad and hula hoops. While Alice was at dancing class from two to three-thirty, I started on an essay which I tried to finish after she'd gone to bed. I had neither the time nor the energy for socialising.

However, at exactly eleven o'clock the next morning, both of us neatly dressed and one of us slightly nervous, we were at Dilys's front door.

Before I'd rung the bell, the door flew open and a small, distracted-looking woman rushed past us. 'Take your mum in, Alice, I won't ...' she called over her shoulder, as she rushed down the path and into the road.

Why was Dilys's mother rushing out in such a hurry? As soon as we'd arrived?

She was dressed in a way I associated with punk teenagers,

no safety pins as far as I could see, but short spikey hair and a black garment with zips. My mouth was suddenly dry.

Alice dragged me into the sitting-room and immediately switched on the television. 'Oh Alice,' I began to say, but stopped abruptly. The room was like a crowded junk shop, several pretty tables, half a dozen very dainty papier mâché chairs and, in contrast, three or four oversized chests of drawers, a pub piano and a seven-foot-long leather settle which looked as though it had been thrown out – and not before time – from a station waiting-room. I sat on a Victorian nursing chair, covered in the original velvet with the genuine Victorian stains, feeling more and more uncomfortable.

I was about to make a decision to leave, when two small boys, a few sizes smaller than Alice, wandered in to look me over.

'Hello,' I said. 'What are your names?'

'I'm sure you know,' the older one said amiably. 'because I know your name. It's Sarah Lucas. You're Alice's mother and you're at University.'

'Alice, turn the television off and introduce your friends.'

'She's addicted to it, I'm afraid,' the older boy continued, 'but she'll soon get bored. I'm Gareth and this is my brother, Tom, if you really don't know.'

'Hello,' I said again. 'No, I'm afraid Alice only mentioned Dilys. Where is Dilys?'

'I don't know. Somewhere about. She'll be back soon.'

He seemed to sense my unease. 'Would you like a cup of coffee?' he asked. 'I can make coffee. Or would you like some tea?'

The little one didn't intend to be outdone. 'Or would you like some Mozart?' he asked, clambering up on to one of the chests of drawers and riffling through a cardboard box. 'Vivaldi,' he read out, 'Elgar, Bach, Brahms. What does this say, Gar?'

'Stravinsky, you dope.'

'Stravinsky, Bach, Elgar, Mozart, Mozart. This is the one you want.'

He snatched it up and put it on the record player, turning the

136

volume high, to drown the noise of the television.

'Quartet for oboe and strings, Küchel 370,' Gareth said. 'That dope's addicted to the oboe.'

He leaned against me. I could smell his little-boy smell, warm and musty like the inside of biscuit tins. He might be precocious, but he smelled as sweet and stale as any other little boy. I wanted to hug him, but of course I didn't.

Tom, pretty as a little monkey, was staring at me from the top of the chest. 'I've got a Sarah at my school,' he said, 'but she's not a good girl.' He sighed extravagantly as he thought of her. Then he brightened up. 'Sometimes I'm very good. Sometimes I say, please may I.'

'Sometimes you're a dope,' Gareth said.

It was another three or four minutes before their mother returned. 'Hello, Sarah, I'm Dilys,' she said. (This was Alice's little friend!) 'And this, heaven help us, is Maudie.'

She handed a squirming something to Gareth who put it down his shirt. 'Take her back upstairs, love, or she'll get out again,' she said. 'I'm sorry I was so long, Sarah. I got her straightaway, but I had to stop and have a little chat with the old boy next door. (This was Colonel Simpson – now dead – who never spoke to anyone.) He loves white rats, bless him. Had one when he was a boy. Oh Sarah, I'm so glad you came over. I've heard so much about you from Alice. Why don't we have a drink to celebrate our first meeting? And then I'll pop down to Sid's to get us all some fish and chips.'

She held my upper arm and pressed it and I looked into her clear green eyes. And in that moment I knew she was going to be the friend I'd always longed for and never had: Dilys.

We all became aware, at the same moment it seems, of the silence in the room. What are the others thinking of? 'It's a lousy day,' Jack says, going to stand by the window again.

I make a small sound in my throat as I try to respond. It's such a bad day for me that the weather simply doesn't count. If

I knew Alice was safe it could blow gales and typhoons and tornadoes.

'Doesn't feel like a Monday,' Dilys says, making an effort to appear her normal, bright self. 'I'm usually rushing about like a mad thing on a Monday.' She whistles the chorus of 'Dashing away with a Smoothing Iron'.

It sounds rather desperate.

'I do my washing on a Sunday,' Jack says, 'before getting the kids back from Lena. I take over two machines at the Victoria Street launderette and finish the *Observer* while I'm waiting. Best part of the week. I don't do any ironing.'

As though we haven't noticed.

'Stevie sometimes complains about her dresses being wrinkled, so I hang them in front of the radiator for a while and that seems to satisfy her.'

'I love ironing,' Dilys says. 'I do it when I'm watching rubbish on the telly. Two lovely things.'

'Don't you have any help in the house?' I ask Jack. 'Why not?'

'Good Lord, no. The house runs itself. I don't know what people are always complaining about. We've got a dish-washer. Fred hoovers sometimes. Twenty pence a carpet. What else is there? I go to the WI market Friday lunchtime and buy some home-made cakes and pies. Great value.'

'My Auntie Dolly is a pillar of the WI,' Dilys says. 'She's in their official cookery book. South Glamorgan. Mrs Dorothea Jones's apple and bran buns. She's famous.'

'If you've got a dish-washer, why don't you get a washing machine?' I ask. 'Why bother to go to the launderette?'

'Lena took the washing machine. Perhaps I'll get one next year.'

'You had the children,' I say, 'so surely you should have had the washing machine.'

I must be in a bad way to get so worked up about other people's domestic arrangements.

Dilys notices my voice getting shrill.

'I hope there's a little sink somewhere in heaven,' she says. 'For my mother. Otherwise she won't be happy. She never got on with the Hoovermatic I bought her. To tell the truth, she never really got on with detergents. Oxydol was what she liked, a block of green soap for the collar and cuffs and then a good boil. Her sheets were beautiful, I'll say that. If they'd brought my father home dead from a pit accident, she wouldn't have had to feel ashamed.'

I get up and go an stand by the window. I know Dilys is trying to take my mind off Alice, but I can't appreciate it.

'David phoned Sarah earlier on,' Dilys says. 'David Noel-Smith. Wanted to see her. No wonder she's in a state.'

'I'm in a state because my daughter's missing and may be in danger. I've hardly given David a thought.'

Dilys, stung by the anger in my voice, says nothing.

It's Jack who replies. 'Good,' he says. 'Don't see him again.'

I stare at him, amazed at his daring. 'What? Why not? What business is it of yours?'

'Because you're getting over him. You've been looking much better lately, much less tense, and your lessons are almost—'

'My *lessons*? My *lessons* are what?'

'Oh God, what have I said now? I shouldn't listen to your lessons, I know, but I have a private-study period with 5M on Friday morning and you're in the next room so I can't help over-hearing you. Back in September, October, you weren't yourself at all, but now you're back on form. That's all I meant.'

'Back on form?'

He shrugs his shoulders. 'In the autumn, you couldn't care less. Then round February, March, you rallied. That's all I meant. It seemed as though you'd started to get over him.'

'That's right,' Dilys says. 'She has rallied. She's become stronger and more self-sufficient. I've noticed it myself. What she needs now is—'

'What I need now is some peace and quiet,' I say. 'For God's sake, leave me alone.'

'I think people have left you alone too long,' Jack says, very

139

quietly and calmly. 'By this time, you need new people and new interests. Listen, I know what it is to lose someone. It does seem the end of the world; too much to bear. But you have to bear it. You have to fill every minute of your time with all sorts of trivial things, and, honestly, among all the dull and pretentious people you come up against, there'll be a few who'll interest you, and before too long, one or two who'll begin to mean something to you. And when that happens, you're halfway to being cured. Honestly.'

'She knows all that as well as you do,' Dilys says. 'God, that was what she was prescribing for Peter.'

'Nobody else interests me. Nobody else means anything.'

'They will,' Jack says. 'Give it a try. Please.'

Chapter 16

I dream I'm being burned alive; Saint Joan or someone.

I wake to find the sun high in the sky and the car like an oven smelling of the new nylotex upholstery.

Peter is asleep, his face helpless and gentle, his lips blurred as though with kissing.

Pity is what I feel for him. Even seeing my ruined leather jacket on the floor at my feet arouses none of the passionate hatred I'd felt earlier.

I open the window, but there's no breeze and I prefer to suffer the heat than risk waking him by opening a door. I hope he'll sleep for a good long while yet. I'm not looking forward to our next confrontation. I have to admit that I consider slipping out of the car, locking him in and scuttling off to find help, but finally decide it would be too cruel, too like another betrayal. (Why another betrayal? Do I feel I've already betrayed him? When? How come? I've always been absolutely honest with him, never pretending I meant anything permanent or even semi-permanent.)

When will someone come past?

It's almost midday and I'm cramped, thirsty and desperate for a pee. All I can do is look around me and try to stay calm.

The lane is narrow and muddy with ragged hedges on either side. The sky is a fresh blue with little fluffy clouds rushing across it like a flock of Persil-dipped sheep.

I decide that the large tree behind us is a sycamore.

I'm not very good at painting trees. I aim at a sort of distant haze of blue-greens and fawns with some delicate squiggles to indicate leaves. Gainsborough used the same technique.

Seriously though, I may do some painting from life in this next year. The way the light falls on those leaves stabs me in the heart.

Oh shut up. I bet Cezanne didn't talk about things stabbing him in the heart. He just noted things. Coolly. OK, some of those leaves are copper-coloured and the ones underneath, slate-blue, not one of them is green, they're all separate and individual and yet they all come together without a break. And yes, they stab me in the heart, too.

Could I become a woman with a tweed hat and hunting-stick, spending my time doing water colours? Well, I just might, if I could find the right hat. A large Christopher-Robin sou'wester in a chicken-paté-coloured Irish tweed and at least fifty years old. With a distinguished label. Also a cape, sweeping the ground, black turning pond-green, in that soft, woollen material that takes on a velvety sheen when it's out in the rain. I've got the exact shoes, men's brogues – I take a seven – in an autumn-bracken, red squirrel-brown.

The woods are lovely, dark and deep. But I have promises to keep. And miles to go before I sleep. Well, Ms Sheila Burton MA, there's your quotation, and I didn't even have to search for it. Very apt i'faith. But have I promises to keep? Of course not. No-one would care a fart whether I took that job or not. In fact, one of the other three or four on the shortlist would be highly delighted.

Have I got it in me, though, to give myself over to trying to be an artist? Am I willing to dig down to the deepest depths of myself to produce something that I'm seeing with my own eyes, not with anyone else's? Something that's true and unaffected? Everyone says I've got a good sense of colour and composition, but most people who've been at it for three years manage to acquire those basics. How do I know whether I've got the extra thing? Colour and composition are only like the rhythm and rhymes of a poem. It's the something else that makes you hold your breath. And is it something you *can* acquire, however hard you work, however deep you mine?

What a complicated life is this I lead. I could certainly do without Brother Peter here.

I turn towards him and find him awake and staring at me.

'Hello, friend,' I say.

'Alice. I killed my mother,' he says.

Bloody hell. I take a deep breath and another look at the great sycamore, or possibly hornbeam, lime; I'm suddenly less sure about everything. 'Peter,' I say, 'I think you're just trying to impress me. But honestly, I found *The Playboy* one of the most boring plays of the Western World, and anyway the line is "I killed my da'." Try it again.'

'I killed my mother,' he says.

I take another deep breath. Tragedy is the last thing I can face. Especially with an empty stomach and a full bladder. God, what am I doing here?

'She wouldn't let me phone you,' he says.

I whistle through my teeth. This guy always manages to get me on the raw. I haven't felt so helpless for years.

He looks deeply into my eyes. 'Why couldn't you have left me alone last night? I knew what to do last night.'

I try to pull myself together. 'You'll thank me one day, Peter. I know you will.'

'I only wanted to speak to your mother. Only wanted her to give you my love. And to tell you I was sorry. I didn't want to speak to you. Christ, how I wish I hadn't phoned.'

'I'm glad you did. It was Fate. Look, I'd only that minute walked into the house. It was Fate.'

'Where had you been? For a whole month?'

'In Rome.'

'In Rome?' He bends forward so that he can look into my eyes. 'Oh, why didn't you stay there? Why did you have to come back?'

I'm suddenly angry again. 'Because I heard about you and Dilys, that's why.'

There's a long silence. He looks sullen rather than ashamed, a schoolboy caught cheating. I seem to be much more upset than he is.

'Why did you do it? What could have got into you?'

In spite of myself, my voice cracks a bit, and he looks at me with such surprise. As though he can't believe that I'm really upset by what happened, as though he thinks I'm beyond feeling pity or sympathy or love.

'I'm not going to talk about it because you've already made up your mind. You've already decided it was rape. That I raped her. If she hadn't been your mother's friend, would you have been so ready to turn against me?'

'I haven't turned against you. If I had I wouldn't be here now, would I?'

'You believe her.'

'Yes, I believe her. But I'm ready to believe you as well, up to a point.'

'What does that mean? Up to a point?'

'You thought she was leading you on. I believe that much.'

He seems surprised that I'm prepared to allow him even that.

'Alice, she taunted me. Said you'd never loved me. Said you'd had an abortion, that you'd have nothing more to do with me.'

I'm a feminist. I shouldn't be feeling sorry for this thug. What if he'd *killed* Dilys? She's one of my friends, one of my best friends. God, I think I'm going mad as well. It's bloody catching.

'So you became violent towards her? Raped her?'

'No, I didn't rape her. It was just that she was ... well, she was more or less saying that I hadn't satisfied you and never could, more or less saying ... oh, I don't know.'

'You felt she was challenging you?'

'She was.'

144

'Making assumptions about your performance? The size of your prick? What?'

'She was standing in front of me in such a provocative way, it could only have meant one thing.'

'Oh sure! There she was, this female creature with legs and, God damn it, two breasts, and looking at you and breathing.'

'Don't mock me. You know I'm not a violent person. You know that much about me.'

'I don't. You've just been telling me that you killed your mother.'

He's mad, all right. As soon as I mention his mother, he becomes a little boy again, a little simpering boy.

'She was so kind, Alice. She kept on saying I wasn't to blame, that I'd got into bad company, that I wasn't to blame myself. All the way back in the train, she was talking about how I used to help her when I was little, the things I used to do for her. She kept on trying to boost my morale. You know, reminding me about all the school prizes I'd had and the cups for public speaking. She said she often wondered whether I might still decide to go in for the Church.'

She would. Oh God, why doesn't someone come to rescue me from this madman?

'Go on,' I say, trying to keep my voice calm and friendly.

'When we got home, there was a sort of family gathering. My brothers were there and my father of course, and they all seemed so sympathetic. I felt they were all behind me, that they understood the strain I'd been under, so that whatever I had to go through, I'd have their full support. They knew I wasn't capable of rape, that the charges against me had been brought by a jealous, scheming woman.'

'Dilys? Yes, I recognise her by that description. An actress too, don't forget, and twice-divorced and very probably suffering from pre-menstrual tension. Oh, you've got nothing whatsoever to worry about, Peter. You'll have everybody on your side.'

The silence between us is hard as stone.

145

I have to bring him down to earth. 'You were telling me about your mother. The reason you attacked her.'

He turns his head away.

'We had some supper,' he mumbles.

'Go on. You had some supper. Did your father say grace first? I'm just trying to picture it.'

'I tried to eat – it was cold meat and salad – but I couldn't. Even though I hadn't had anything all day. I couldn't seem to swallow.'

'Well, go on. Did your mother make you sit there until you'd eaten every mouthful? Even the beetroot?'

'She said she'd get me some soup, and I did manage to eat a little of that.'

'Cream of chicken?'

He pauses for a moment. 'I think it was as a matter of fact. Why? What does it matter?'

'The small details are very important. Cream of chicken is a great standby.'

'Afterwards I helped her wash up. It was just her and me. And then she said I should have an early night, that she had a sleeping tablet I could have.'

He grinds to a stop again. He's very pale.

I prompt him. 'And then you said you wanted to contact me? To phone my mother?'

He puts his forehead on the car window. He tries to say something but fails.

'Stupid fuckin' woman,' I say, quite forgetting that I'm speaking about someone who's supposed to be dead.

He turns towards me, and with no sort of warning, clouts me hard across the face.

'Stupid fuckin' woman,' I say again. My nose is bleeding and all my front teeth feel loose. 'Stupid fuckin' woman,' I shout at him, shaking my head so that great dollops of blood spurt about everywhere. Stupid fuckin' woman, I'm thinking. The back of my throat tastes of metal polish.

'Well, I'm going,' I say, when I've hammed it up as much as

I can and the flow seems to be drying up. 'I'll faint if I stay here. Are you coming with me or not?'

'Don't leave me,' he says. God, he's a broken-down wreck again.

'It's too hot in here, and we need something to eat. I'm going to walk on to the nearest house. Are you coming with me?'

'We were shouting at one another, and she was pulling the phone away from me. And I could hear my father coming from the study to see what it was all about. And I got hold of this storage jar, a heavy stone jar, and I hit her on the head with it, and she fell forward on to the draining board, and then I picked up a knife and got away from them. My father and my brothers were there by that time. And I heard my father say, "Oh Eileen. Oh my God." And I ran out.'

'Oh Peter, she's not dead. How can you be so daft? People don't die as easily as that. She might have been knocked unconscious, but she's long recovered by this time. People don't die when they're hit on the head with a jar.'

I met his mother on one awful occasion and she didn't strike me as the kind of woman you could kill with a single blow on the head. Or with a single bomb, come to that.

'My God, if you think killing people is as easy as that, you should be in the fuckin' army. I'll phone your father to find out how she is. I bet you a hundred quid she's OK. Stop worrying about her. Look, let's be on our way. Before we're too weak to walk.'

'I'm not going anywhere.'

'Oh Peter, no-one's going to find us here.'

'I don't want anyone to find us.'

'You want to starve to death, is that it? Listen, kid, I feel very sorry for you, I really do. You've got yourself in a right old mess, I'm not denying that, and I'd play it your way if it was humanly possible. But it isn't. It's almost half past twelve and I haven't had breakfast yet, and I didn't have a meal yesterday except for a tiny snack on the plane. I'm starving.'

He takes hold of one of my wrists and grips it hard. I try not to wince, to tell myself that it's only old Peter.

'Did you have an abortion?' he asks, his voice like a butcher's knife.

'It was a false alarm, Peter. I didn't need to. It was OK.'

He tightens his grip. 'I don't believe you. You *were* pregnant. You were drooping every morning and white as a ghost. I know you had an abortion. You must have. You did.'

He throws my wrist back at me – I examine the marks of his nails on it – and then slumps back on to the seat.

Very calmly, and without saying another word, I get out. I turn to look at him as I'm closing the door; he's watching me as though he doesn't care what I do.

Can someone commit suicide, I wonder, in a car which has run out of petrol? My insides are still churning about. I open the door again but he won't look at me.

'Listen, Peter, I'm still your friend, right? I'm not going to marry you. I'm not even going to be your lover again. That part's over. But I'm still your friend. Right? And you can count on that. Whatever happens, whatever you've done. Right? I'm not a good person, as you tell me so often: I steal from supermarkets when I'm hungry and I lie as often as I tell the truth. But, as for you, I still happen to think that you're a better person than most. So I'm going to try to overlook your totally uncharacteristic outbursts of violence – even your attack on me. Hold on to that, right? You're not alone, kid, I'm with you. Right?'

He makes absolutely no reply, doesn't even look at me.

So I leave the car again, and after answering a call of nature – as my grandmother used to say – start walking towards what I hope will be a not-too-distant farmhouse; I can see plenty of car and tractor marks on the hardened mud.

As a result of my passionate and not entirely ignoble speech, I'm on a high for quite a long time. (Unfortunately, Peter didn't seem at all affected by it. That's life, I suppose.) I make a determined effort not to think about him – that way madness lies – but about myself. I run my fingers through my hair and wonder what I look like, what impression I'll make on the people at the farm. Where is the damned place? I try to imagine kindly people anxious to do all they can to help me: a large, white-haired farmer who'll get out his Range Rover to fetch Peter; a plump middle-aged farmer's wife who'll run me a bath and get me a woolly vest and a hand-knitted jumper-suit (maroon) and a steaming cup of hot chocolate. Where is the damned farm?

I start to think about breakfast: lovely fresh bread, warm and dusted with flour; crisp, buttery croissant; bitter continental-blend coffee, or Lapsang Souchong tea tasting faintly of kippers; marmalade; Cooper's Oxford, and Sainsbury's Thick Cut; oh, and apples, ripening slowly in a misty autumn morning, English apples with their manly English names – Egremont's Russet, Lord Lambourne, Charles Ross, James Grieve, and Cox's Orange Pippin, boxes and boxes of them, individually wrapped for the Christmas market. I can smell the bloody things. And I can smell fresh bread, too, and grilled bacon and mushrooms. Oh, mushrooms!

I must have walked two miles before the rain starts; two miles without sign of a house or habitation. I didn't realise there were such isolated spots in this corner of industrial England.

The rain begins to fall heavily, softening the mud and making walking difficult. Once again I curse Peter; my torn jacket is being blown apart by a sudden wind and my back is getting soaked. God, I'm getting completely drenched. Drenched, what a super word. For a while I trudge along, repeating it under my breath.

A thunder storm is the next thing, a ferocious bloody thunder storm. The sky's become a shiny dark-purple like hot blackberry jam, and torrents of rain come down like frenzied plastic sheets.

I'm helpless. The wind and rain beat against me in whatever direction I turn, so that I can't move, or even stand upright.

I crouch down on the verge of the lane, where there's squelching mud rather than swirling water and put my head in my lap. There's suddenly thunder crashing immediately above me and streaks of lightning whipping across the sky. This must be a hurricane.

Or is it the end of the world?

No. Like Noah before me, I live to tell the tale. After about five minutes, the rain slackens and the thunder rumbles away and I lift bands of wet hair off my face, squeeze out the front of my Italian T-shirt, wipe my muddy hands on a clump of emerald-green grass – the light is fantastic – and carry on walking, splashing through enormous puddles like a toddler in new red wellingtons.

I must buy some new red wellingtons.

I look at my watch. Thirteen-thirty.

I start worrying about my mother. What did she do when she found my bed empty? She's got enough on her plate with Dilys. Wherever does she think I've got to?

'I don't worry as long as I know where you are,' she used to say when I was fifteen, sixteen. I could never understand how the knowledge comforted her, since I could – and did – get up to all sorts of depravity at a Church fête.

She used to send me to Dilys's every Wednesday evening, because that was when 'Uncle' David used to visit her for the weekly treat, and she didn't think I should be around in case their mad, reeling passion – I don't think – should enflame my adolescent breast. Her excuse was that Dilys needed me to baby-sit for her, and this meant that for about two years poor Dilys had to go out every Wednesday night, whether she wanted to or not.

Anyway, this gave me a great opportunity to get on with my own life. (I simply couldn't work up an interest in the Sixth-Form boys Mum encouraged me to bring home; they talked too much and were always so keen to *explain* things to me.)

My first real affair was with an eighteen-year-old road mender, with a thick mane of tawny-coloured hair and thick gold-tanned arms. Even his eyes were golden. He always arrived on the dot of nine, but I could never persuade him to stay for much more than an hour; he was probably terrified of being discovered with me. He didn't talk much. Perhaps he felt awkward at being in such a strange house – Dilys's place is full of silk cushions and parasols and copper pots and imitation parrots in wicker cages – perhaps I didn't interest him much, except for the first mad tussle on the settee or the Persian rug. I remember his showing me how to fill in football pools, though, and assuring me that Tottenham Hotspur was the best team in the world, even when they were losing.

He carried on coming for months – so did I – though I never saw him except for those Wednesday evenings. He was always on his dignity, very proud of his hard muscles and his golden sideburns which he used to comb and pat into place before leaving.

One Wednesday he failed to turn up, but kindly sent a mate along with a note. 'Sorry to have to inform you that our association must now close. George Stokes.'

Upset as I was, I was still able to admire the style and brevity of that letter; I've often been tempted to adapt it for my own use, but have never quite had the nerve.

I've never seen him since, though I never pass any road works without looking out for him.

Perhaps he's married by this time, with one or two tawny cubs.

Ellie Stephenson is married with a three-month-old baby girl, and she's almost a year younger than me. She used to be so wild, too, always in trouble for sniffing glue and carpet clearners. She was the first in our form to have a nose stud, and now she pushes a pram and wears an anorak.

I wonder if I'll ever settle down with anyone? I'd like to, in a way. Could I ever commit myself to one person, though? Whoever I'm with, I find myself watching somebody else, trying to arouse his interest. There are so many thrilling possibilities, how can anyone be prepared to pass them by? I look at men and hanker and lust, but don't know how to create any decent lasting love out of it. How to stay in love, that's my problem. Without being shipwrecked by it, like my poor mum. Having some everlasting gut-ache for someone who doesn't have the courtesy to take you seriously can't be right. Can it?

I wonder if Ellie Stephenson is happy. Her baby seemed a chirpy little thing.

I check my watch again. I've been walking for almost an hour and a half. There's a hedge now, at the side of the lane, instead of a fringe of trees, and I climb up to get a better view. There's no sign of a house in any direction and I'm about to get down again, when I'm just in time to see Peter slipping behind a tree about fifty yards back. The idiot has been following me the whole time.

At first, I'm only surprised and angry. Why couldn't he have come with me when I asked him to? Why does he have to hide and make such a mystery of everything? As though everything isn't complicated enough already.

My next feeling is fear. OK, I'm cold and wet and hungry, but the plain fact is that he now looks mad, really demented.

I don't know whether to ignore him and hurry on, or to let him know I've seen him and wait for him to catch me up. And because I'm hesitating instead of thinking what I'm doing, I jump awkwardly, my left foot plunges into a deep rut, there's a pain like a flame, several flames. And I sink down into them.

When I was a kid, I was always in Casualty for something or other: broken arm, leg, collar-bone, but I've never fainted before, never in my whole life. I used to leave that part to my mother.

When I come round, Peter is bending over me, wet as a seal in a dark-grey check jacket, but looking fairly normal again. 'God, you're in a state,' he says. 'What can I do?'

'Help me up, for a start.'

As I try to stand, I almost pass out again; the pain from my ankle is horrific.

'I'll have to carry you,' he says.

'Oh, sure. You'd get very far. Just try to get me back to the hedge, so that I can sit down.'

Even those three hobbling steps are agony.

'I said we should have stayed in the car,' Peter says. 'God knows what we can do now.'

The sky has lightened and the sun appears – honey through

gauze, I try to make a mental note of it – but with no warmth. I can't stop shivering.

Wet, cold, hungry and crippled.

'Do sit down,' I snap at him, 'don't hover. You can't get any wetter. Why were you following me, anyway? Dodging behind trees? Why didn't you call out and come with me?'

'I'll do what I like,' he says truculently, a small boy again.

'I suppose we'll have to stay here now, till someone finds us. Mum will have notified the police by this time and they'll be looking out for us. It can't be long till they come across the car. People are supposed to report abandoned cars, aren't they.'

'I'll see if I can find a house,' Peter says. 'I'll walk on until I reach one and then I'll get someone to phone your mother.'

'Will you really? Oh Peter, thank you.'

I hadn't expected him to co-operate in any way. Perhaps spraining my ankle will turn out a blessing. He looks almost as lively now as when he was threatening to kill me.

'Try not to be too long,' I call after him. 'I feel so bloody feeble sitting here.'

It seems like another world. There's no noise, not even birds, not even aeroplanes, no noise of traffic. I can't believe I'm only five or six miles off the motorway.

The light is greenish and eerie. I never thought I could feel so bloody nervous about being on my own in this country. Or anywhere else for that matter.

God, how long can a person live without food? I saw some unripe blackberries some way back. I wish I'd picked them.

One can eat nettles and dandelion leaves. (*One* can, please note. I very much doubt if *I* can. I can't even eat cabbage.)

Anyway, I know the police will come soon.

Chapter 17

A cloudburst suddenly, with thunder and lightening and whipping winds.

We all three go to stand by the window. It's so dark we can hardly see the houses on the other side of the road.

'I have to do something. I can't take any more of this waiting.' My voice is high like an electric drill. I'm reliving that day when Geoff swam out to sea and I did nothing but wait. Nothing at all to help. Above the noise of the rain and the wind I can hear myself moaning.

'What the hell could you have done?' Dilys says. 'You thought he was safe on another beach.'

'What did I say?' I ask, genuinely worried that Dilys is now reading my thoughts.

'Her husband was drowned at sea,' Dilys tells Jack, 'and of course the silly bitch thinks it was her fault.'

I begin to whine again. 'I must do something. I must do something before it's too late.'

'Come on then,' Jack says, making a move from the window. 'My car's outside. Driving around could be better for us than standing here like dummies. Are you coming, Dilys?'

'No, I suppose I'd better hang on here in case there's a phone call,' she says rather crossly. 'But just give me some idea where you're making for, will you.'

'We'll drive towards the motorway, I suppose,' Jack says.

They exchange glances which I fail to interpret.

'To that Little Chef where she used to meet him off the London coach. Someone may have seen them.'

Dilys and Jack exchange glances again. They think it's a fool's errand. They're humouring me, but I don't care.

Jack's car is right outside but we're wet to the skin by the time we've run down the path. 'Let me drive, Jack. I need something to do, something to occupy my mind. Listen, perhaps you ought to wait with Dilys. She's still very nervous and I'll be fine on my own.'

'No, I'll come with you.'

The car shuddered and leaped as I tried to start it.

'Put your foot hard down on the accelerator a few times before you start the engine. Try again.'

Jack's car was heavy and difficult to drive. I had to give it all my concentration; which was what I needed. For a while, too, conditions were atrocious; it was raining so hard that the wipers could hardly cope. It was like driving under the sea.

'I didn't know your husband had been drowned,' Jack said when we'd gone a couple of miles. 'That must have been hell.'

'Yes.'

'And it explains things, I think.'

'Oh? What sort of things?' I turn and give him a quick half-glance. 'The way I am now, d'you mean?'

'Only that's far too simple an explanation, of course. For the way you are now, I mean. Only perhaps it has some bearing on it . . . Tell me to shut up if you want to.'

'You think the shock of my husband's death made me old before my time? Something like that?'

'You're not old. You don't seem old to me. But perhaps over-cautious. You know, preferring a half-life with someone to . . . daring . . . well, to daring to live fully again.'

Jack's voice had become more and more hesitant as he finished. 'I'm sorry,' he said then. 'I hardly know you. What right have I got to make any comment on the way you are now.'

'You have every right. I invited you to continue.' I tried to speak calmly. 'I suppose there could be some truth in what you say. I'm certainly frightened and nervous a lot of the time.'

'You lost someone you loved. You were afraid to love again.'

'I *did* love again.' My throat is dry, my voice icy. Oh God, and I still love him. I'm in pain. I'm in pain.

'Right.'

'Don't you dare question that.'

'Right. I don't know too much about love, I suppose. Take Peter now. He loved Alice so much it drove him mad.'

'And don't you dare bring Peter into this. How can I bear to think about Peter who may be, even at this moment, threatening my daughter in some way. And don't you dare say that's anything to do with love. Just shut up!'

My voice cracks the air. When was I ever so angry? I can feel anger flooding my veins and bursting into my brain.

'I'm sorry.'

'And don't keep saying you're sorry. You're not sorry. You're trying to goad me.'

'I'm not, believe me.'

'Trying to underestimate how I feel about David Noel-Smith for one thing. Trying to belittle it.'

For a while I drive on in silence. 'Oh, you're very cynical about love, aren't you?' I say then, in an attempt to lighten the air.

'Only the Hollywood sort of love. That sort of love so great and powerful that no-one else and nothing else counts. That's often selfish and rather cruel, it seems to me.'

'I suppose it is sometimes.' But I don't think I was cruel or selfish. I often wish I hadn't sacrificed myself as I did, wish I hadn't had that abortion but had the baby, which would have kept David and me together, at least to some extent. A part of me died when I had that abortion.

'What are you thinking about?'

'I'm worrying that Alice may have had an abortion. Peter thought she had.'

'Are you so against them, then?'

'No. I think women have the right to choose. But it's a painful choice.'

'Are you speaking from experience? I'm sorry, I had no right to ask that . . . But I once thought you had. We were told a minor operation, but I felt it was something else. You looked very lost and vacant for quite a time.'

'I did have an abortion. You're right.' And as far as I know you were the only one who guessed. David never suspected anything. How did you know? 'Jack, I've always misjudged you. To be honest, I think you've rather enjoyed deceiving me. It's a form of power, I suppose. Psychologically speaking.'

'I know less about psychology than I do about love. And what do I think I know about love? All I know can be summed up in a single sentence: I'm all for the sharing, companionable, good-natured sort that makes you happy and doesn't leave you bruised.'

'That's what all of us want. Only that's not how it ends up.'

'And when it gives you more grief than comfort, you should break free.'

'Oh yes! One can be very wise about what other people should do. Even I can manage that.'

We fall silent again. But this time it's Jack who speaks. 'So what should *I* do? Divorce my wife or hang on, hoping for a reconciliation?'

'You're young enough to fall in love again.'

'I'm just four years younger than you.'

'How do you know my age?'

'Alice happened to tell me you were forty-two.'

'How come you were discussing my age with Alice? Oh, it doesn't matter. It's of no importance.' I glance over at him. 'You think something's happened to Alice, don't you? I can tell.'

'No. I feel sure she's OK.'

'Then why are you looking so fraught?'

'I'm slightly nervous, that's all. A car going at sixty in a

158

built-up area always has that effect on me. Specially if I'm in it.'

I slow down. 'I'm sorry. You should have stopped me earlier.'

'I reckoned you needed to use up some of that adrenalin.'

I try to relax, driving in my usual sedate manner until we get to another stretch of countryside. Soon, though, another deluge of rain blinds the windows.

'I'd better stop. I can't see anything at all at the moment.' The road was awash under an inch or two of water.

I try to slow down and we go into a skid, shooting across the mercifully deserted road and into a ditch.

'I'm sorry.'

'That's OK.'

'It hasn't helped matters much, has it? Is there anything I can do? Shall I try reversing?'

'No, just turn the engine off. We won't be able to get out of here without help. You stay here and I'll go to the nearest kiosk to phone a garage.'

'What if the car catches fire?'

'It won't. It's perfectly safe. Down a ditch but otherwise perfectly OK.'

'I think I'd rather go with you.'

'Without a coat?'

'You haven't got a coat. I really don't want to sit here on my own getting more and more nervous and depressed.'

'Right, we'll both go.'

We manage to get out of the car and scramble up to the road. 'I'm very sorry.'

'Now *you're* saying it all the time. It's all right.'

'Anyway, I'll say it once more. I'm very sorry. I've certainly dented your car quite badly and possibly damaged the engine as well. You shouldn't have let me drive.'

'It was all my fault, then. Please accept my apologies.'

I try to smile at him. 'How far do you think we'll have to walk?'

'Not too far. There'll be a kiosk or a pub in the next village. And the rain seems to be stopping.'

'Poor Jack, what a day you're having. What did you intend to do today?'

'Not much. All the sport's been rained off.'

'What do you watch?'

'Cricket, football, rugby, car racing, horse racing, golf, billiards, boxing, darts. Even tennis when there's nothing else. What do you watch? Let me guess. Nature programmes, opera and ballet.'

'You're doing it again.'

'What do you mean?'

'Putting me down. Trying to make out I'm different from other people. You're too hard on me. And don't walk so fast either. You're doing it on purpose.'

He slows down a fraction.

'Don't be angry, Jack. I'll pay for the damage to the car.'

'I don't give a fuck for the damage to the car, as you probably know.'

'I'm sorry.'

'And don't keep saying that.'

'I'm sorry I drove your car into a ditch but I'm not sorry we came out, because I feel much better than when we were stuck in the house just waiting and waiting.'

Jack doesn't answer, but after a moment or two says, 'If by any chance the police drop by when we're having the car winched out of the ditch, I think we'd better say I was driving.'

'Why?'

'Because I don't think I'm as much over the limit as you are.'

We walk on without either of us saying a word.

At last I break the silence. 'Do you really think I'm over the limit?'

'Well, you had a fair few gins, didn't you?'

'You shouldn't have let me drive then, should you?'

'There's a pub sign, look. Thank God for that.'

I sat in the lounge with a lemonade while Jack was phoning.

'You're ever so wet,' the barmaid said. 'There's a towel in the Ladies. You could dry your hair a bit while hubby's phoning. Haven't we had some weather?'

'He's just a friend,' I said. 'He's not my husband.'

'Oh, we don't mind here, love. Anything goes here.'

The couple at the bar turned to look at me and laughed. 'We don't mind, love,' the barmaid said again, making the most of their laughter.

I went to the Ladies. As I dried my face and hair with a far-from-clean roller towel, I stared at myself in the mirror – oval face, large frightened eyes, bedraggled hair – and wondered what Jack really thought of me. Sometimes he seemed to like me. I realised that I certainly liked him. He'd done all he could to help me, far more than I had any right to expect. But there, he always seemed ready to help everyone. I'd always noticed that.

'The bloke at the garage says he'll be there in half an hour,' he said when I got back to the lounge. 'We'll stay here for another ten minutes and then start walking back. The rain seems to have stopped, thank Christ. Do you want to ring Dilys? She'll be glad to know you're safe.'

'Why shouldn't I be safe? No, I don't particularly want to ring her, but you can if you want to. You can tell her what happened and have a little laugh about it.'

He decides to ignore me. 'Drink up,' is all he says. 'Please. You've had a nasty shock.'

'We had an accident in that last downpour,' he tells the barmaid. 'Went straight into a ditch. Couldn't see a bloody thing.'

'You poor thing,' the barmaid says, looking me up and down again. 'Cup of tea you need, love, with two spoons of sugar. I'll make you one.'

I smile at Jack, thanking him for his concern. Inside I'm saying, I'm really sorry we've never got on, Jack. Is it too late to change? You think I'm putting on airs or something, but I'm not. It's just the way I am. Can't we try to accept each other as we are? It's not too late, is it?

I thank the barmaid and gulp down the hot, sweet, sinister-looking tea. Afterwards I feel better than I've felt all day.

Jack puts his arm through mine as we walk back to the car. I'm surprised at how comforting it feels.

Chapter 18

I'm here for what seems like endless ages, my bum on this sodden bank, pints of rainwater tipping down my neck, the pain in my foot excruciating. I try to think of old Turner, lashed to the mast of a ship – what a poseur – observing a storm at sea for some painting or other. All I can observe from here is an ocean of olive-green mud, a putty-coloured sky and some half-grown, diseased-looking alder trees. How long will I be able to stand this?

A few years ago we looked round this dungeon in France; my mother can't seem to pass a castle, I'm the same with ice-cream kiosks. Anyway, this place was cold as a morgue and running with damp and had great rusty leg-irons still clamped to the walls. And the guide – twenty-five francs extra – informed us that some of the prisoners had been kept languishing there for twenty to thirty years.

God, how did they exist even for twenty to thirty days, suffering such agonies of cold, let alone rheumatism and piles and God knows what? Did they spend their time praying? With beads? Endlessly repeating words about love and faith and forgiveness? Did they manage to remember some images from the world outside? The first wisp of new moon, the planes and angles of red-tiled roofs? Or did they spend their time thinking about women? Could they even manage to masturbate, though, on bread and water? But perhaps prisoners in

France had at least half-decent meals, something like our school dinners, but with lots of garlic. At the moment I could eat a floorcloth if it was sautéed in olive oil and garlic; I'd give my miserable soul for some cream of asparagus cup-a-soup – my stomach is growling like a puppy.

I start thinking of the little restaurant in Rome where Charlie used to take me.

It was rather a gloomy place, the walls painted a dark-red like raw liver, a flagstone floor, no music, and waiters who were all old and ugly.

At first I was disappointed that he hadn't taken me to a smarter, glossier place. But as soon as they brought us the food, I was more than satisfied. I think we ate and drank for two or three hours.

I can't stop myself going over those courses, one by one.

I wonder if I could get hold of a recipe and learn to cook that wonderfully rich pasta sauce, made with mussels and shallots and spinach – or was it seaweed – absolutely super anyway, with masses of wine and cream, I suppose.

When I did cookery at school, we only made things like soda scones and walnut cake.

Not that there's anything wrong with soda scones and walnut cake.

Not that there's anything wrong with fresh granary bread and a bar of milk chocolate. Expensive, but OK for a main meal. Fresh granary bread. Milk chocolate . . .

Oh joy and joy without end. There's a car, a big black Rover, coming slowly down the lane towards me.

Even before it stops and proceeds to do a fifteen-point turn, I can see that the driver is none other than my companion of the night, Peter Roderick Anthony Venables. Even this doesn't depress me too much.

'Have you rung my mother?' I ask, as he comes out to help me into the car.

'Yes,' he says.

'Is she OK?'

'Yes,' he says. 'She's fine.'

'Where did you get the car?'

'It's the farmer's. He's milking, so he couldn't come himself.'

He drives for about a minute and a half, then pulls up at a small square dolls' house right at the edge of the lane.

'They've got a cup of tea waiting for you,' he says.

He helps me up the path – three painful steps – and opens the door.

Then he carries me over the threshold and puts me into an easy chair. 'This is the living-room,' he says.

'Where are they?' I ask, looking round me and easing off my boot, as he goes back to close the door.

He goes into the kitchen, instead of answering.

'The kettle's boiled and I've got you some tea and cake,' he says after a moment or two.

'So where's the bloody farmer?' I shout at him, suddenly very angry and suspicious. 'This doesn't look like a farmhouse to me, mate. This looks like Red Riding Hood's cottage, this does. Her grandmother's cottage in the dark wood.'

He puts a cup of tea on a little table by my side. His breathing is heavy.

I look him in the eye. 'Have you rung my mother?' I ask.

'No,' he says.

I pick up the cup of lovely hot tea and throw it at him, watching with interest as his white shirt turns a yellowy-brown and starts steaming. He clutches at it, pulling it away from his chest, and then goes rushing back to the kitchen.

I hobble to the front door.

It's locked, of course, and the key's in his damned pocket.

The three bears' cottage has a nasty black lock, kiddies, and anyway Goldilocks has hurt her footsy-wootsy and can't run away . . . Or go to the fuckin' ball.

So what the bloody hell will she do now?

Well, she mops up some tears – of rage, not despair – with a towel thoughtfully provided earlier by Daddy Bear, limps to the chair, rams a piece of sponge cake into her mouth, swallows hard and prepares to wait.

There's much running of water from the kitchen and behind that, the lowing of cows, sounding fairly close. Perhaps there is a farm and a farmer somewhere around.

Peter comes back with a red and white check tea-cloth on instead of a shirt. Even this fails to cheer me up.

'Would you like some water to bathe your foot?' he asks in a quiet voice.

I refuse to answer or look at him.

'I have to return the car to the farm,' he says after a minute or two.

I struggle to my feet. 'I'll come with you.'

'There's no need.'

'Won't they think it odd that you haven't got out of your wet clothes?'

'All I have to do is return it to the garage.'

'Won't they expect you to call in to thank them?'

'No. I said we were on our honeymoon.'

I let that sink in.

'When you've gone, I'll break the window and scream.'

'They won't hear you.'

'They might.'

'Try it if you like, but for God's sake don't get glass in your hand.'

He goes out. I hop to the kitchen, a tiny room with nothing much in it but a sink – where his shirt is soaking, what a good little housewife he is – a cooker and a cupboard. On the cupboard door there's a list of instructions about the electricity meter, the cooker and the immersion heater, and a warning about not putting nappy-pads or any foreign bodies (underlined) – who the hell's been here? – down the lavatory.

It must be a holiday cottage. Christ, we're honeymooners in a holiday cottage and they'll leave us alone all week.

Inside the cupboard, with the dishes, there's a small cardboard

166

box with some food; a loaf, cheese, butter and tea, but my appetite's completely gone.

There's some cutlery in a drawer. I suppose I could get one of the windows open if I really tried, but I'm too tired and my foot aches too much. I'll do it tomorrow, if I must.

I haul myself up the steep, red-carpeted staircase and get to a pretty little cottage bedroom with sloping ceiling and double bed and next to it a tiny bathroom with a half-size bath and a lav. There's no sign of a farmhouse through the matchbox-size windows of either room, nothing but woods and rough fields and from the back window, a straight hedge which might mark a road.

I use the lavatory and run water for a bath. The water is warm but soon runs cold. Never mind, even a cool bath will be better than nothing. I lock the door – two can play at this game – peel off my wet clothes and get into the bath. My foot feels worse instead of better, the water is hard and there's no soap, not even a sliver, but I try to relax to plan my next move.

After a few minutes, I hear Peter return. He calls me, but I don't answer. He bounds upstairs and rattles the door.

'Alice,' he says. I don't even breathe.

'Alice. Alice.'

The poor bastard's in a panic again. Does he think I've managed to drown myself? He probably hasn't seen the size of the bath.

Now he's trying to break down the door.

I get out of the water as quietly as I can and unlock it, so that he practically falls into the room.

Mercy me, he's crying again. He sinks to his knees sobbing. The water is quite cold by the time he manages to speak.

'Alice, I was *going* to phone your mother. Honestly. That's all I intended when I got to the farm. I swear to you. I had everything worked out, what I was going to say, I mean. Everything ready.'

'OK. So what happened?' My voice is colder than the bathwater.

'They have people to stay. Bed and breakfast. And they took it for granted, I wanted bed and breakfast. And before I could explain, they said they were full up for the next couple of weeks, but that the cottage was vacant. There'd been a last-minute cancellation. And they said what a nice cottage it was, how they always laid on milk and eggs and a few necessities. And without really thinking about it, I said it would be fine. I had to give them ten pounds deposit, and when I told them about the car, they said I could take theirs to fetch you. The chap even said he'd bring me a gallon of petrol when he'd finished the milking.'

'I see. And what are you hoping to gain from this nasty little episode? We're not honeymooners or even lovers. I've told you that's over. So what are you hoping for? All you're doing is making me despise you. Even more than I do already.'

I get out of the bath and try to dry myself with the small kitchen towel he'd brought me earlier.

'Is there another towel? If there is, will you please fetch it?'

I'm shivering with cold and anger.

He goes downstairs and brings me another, not much bigger than a pocket handkerchief. 'That's all there is,' he says.

'Right. Now go straight back to the farm and ask them for some First Aid stuff. I've broken a bone in my foot. Look how swollen it is. What clothes am I going to put on? Do you expect me to put these things back on? Even my bra and pants are wet through.'

I show him my T-shirt – my beautiful silk T-shirt – which is like a sodden dishcloth. To emphasise the point, I clean the bath with it.

'There's an electric fire. We can put the electric fire on and dry them.' His voice is thick with misery.

'And what do I do in the meantime? Can you produce a nice warm fluffy dressing-gown for me to put on? Listen, you'd better go to phone my mother, hadn't you.'

I push him out of the way and hobble to the bedroom. My foot is still agony, but the bed is comfortable, a good firm mattress and a summer-weight duvet.

'Try to dry my clothes,' I say. 'And bring me some bread and butter and some tea. And then go to ring my mother. Please.'

My voice has softened again. After all, he's wet to the gills as well and he looks pretty stupid with a red and white check tea-cloth draped round his shoulders instead of a shirt.

'Oh go away,' I say. 'For God's sake, just go away.'

Chapter 19

After her ordeal in Jack's car, Sarah begged me to stay with her last night. I slept in Alice's room, her paraphanalia; posters and photographs, dresses and jewellery, make-up and perfume all around me, so perhaps it's not surprising that I had a series of vivid dreams about her.

She and I were in some sort of festival, a great gathering of noisy hippies in long black dresses and ragged jeans; some singing, some dancing, some with guitars, with bands playing too loudly in various tents in the background. I was uneasy, conscious of some tragedy – a death? – which the others, including Alice, didn't seem ready to face. At last there was some sort of silence, with people carrying a coffin towards us. Then I spotted my Uncle Ifor emerging out of the crowd, his dark-grey Sunday suit and white shirt immaculate. I was relieved to see him, knowing that he'd get things properly organised, restoring everyone to a respectful silence and getting some decent hymn-singing started.

'Have you learnt the piece?' he asked me.

'What piece? No-one asked me to learn anything.'

'Aren't you *the actress*?' he asked with unconcealed sarcasm. And then, 'You were given weeks to learn it.'

The crowd was suddenly quiet, waiting for me to begin. I was terrified, feeling my heart pounding, my throat drying up. People started clapping, very slowly and rhythmically.

'Just go up to the platform and begin,' my Uncle Ifor said.

'Come with me,' I begged Alice, but she only laughed at me and shook her head. And turned away from me and walked into the crowd.

It was an enormous relief to wake up.

But I was soon tossing and turning again: why hadn't I managed to learn the damned thing, whatever it was? Was this an omen? Was I, from now on, going to be incapable of learning any small part I might be offered?

And why was Uncle Ifor in my dream? I hadn't seen him for at least five years. Wasn't it ever possible to get away from one's family and one's background? Still sweating with agitation I fell asleep again.

Another dream. A clearing in the forest, early spring, beech trees bare against an enamelled blue sky, young green grass underfoot. This time Alice was driving me slowly along a woodland track in Sarah's new car. Suddenly I asked her to stop; I'd noticed some willow catkins which I thought Sarah might like.

I walked back along the muddy track. The catkins were yellow and fluffy, their pollen showering over me as I picked them. The tighter, silvery ones were too high up for me to reach.

As I was about to give up, I could see a man coming along the path towards me and wondered if he'd help me pick some from the higher branches. But when I asked him he only grinned salaciously and lunged towards me, throwing me over on to the soft muddy ground. He was so strong that I couldn't move. I screamed for Alice and could see her getting out of the car, but all she did was stand there, holding the door, leaning on it. I shouted again, but realised that she was laughing at me; laughing in an exaggerated, excited way, her whole body shaking, as though she was getting some hideous sexual gratification from seeing the stranger assaulting me. It was horrible. It was obscene.

I woke up sweating, the sheet I'd had over me coiled round and round me as though I'd been wrestling with it. My heart was thumping, hurting my ribs, as it had after the actual rape. It was difficult to breathe.

172

What disturbed me most was the thought that Alice might be taking it lightly – I mean, the actual rape. I had no way of knowing whether she was on my side or not. I couldn't bear to think that her sympathies were with Peter. Sarah had assured me that Alice felt exactly as she did, but Sarah would have been more anxious to comfort me than tell the plain truth.

I love Alice. She's been as close as a daughter to me for over fifteen years and I can't bear to think that anything might come between us. I honestly think that, for good or bad – bad probably – I've been the greatest influence on Alice's life. She was always devoted to her mother, but wanted to be completely different from her, so that I became her role-model. Sarah was too self-effacing, too forgiving, too reasonable, whereas I was ruthless, rude, loud, assertive. Even when she was nine or ten she'd stamp her foot in exactly the way I did: 'Now listen to me, all of you. I'm the boss.' She adopted all my least attractive mannerisms and the worst of my vocabulary. I know I shouldn't have been pleased, but I was. And somehow Sarah tolerated all her most brazen behaviour. I took her home with me once to be company for Tom when Gareth was in Scouts' camp, and my mother couldn't get over what a little loud-mouth she was. '*Someone* hasn't been taught any manners,' she said. '*Someone* has been dragged up, I'm afraid,' (My father used to clout us if we as much as muttered crickey or heck.)

Alice loved being in my home; loved the attention she got from all the family – all my uncles and aunties. 'Her mother's a *teacher*,' my mother used to whisper to them, trying to make up for Alice's lapses in decorum. (Teachers were still highly respected in my home, in the social scale only slightly below doctors, preachers and Labour MPs.) She also loved the huge meals she had three times a day with snacks of home-made chips and bread-and-butter and tea when anyone came to call. The thing she liked best of all was my mother's gravy. In cookery books, gravy is described as the meat juices from which the fat has been separated, but cookery books are usually written by middle-class English ladies. In South Wales, gravy is substantial;

a substitute for the second slice of meat. All the fat is left in the meat-tin with the juices, flour is added, just the right amount to take up the fat, then vegetable water until it reaches the perfect, thick, shiny consistency. My father and all my uncles liked gravy even on chips or sausages. So did Alice. And still does. She still supports Wales in rugby internationals too.

That lovely friendly relationship we've always had, I can't bear to think it may be over. Obviously, the overwhelming admiration she had for me is long past, she sees me now for what I am, but I don't want her to scorn or pity me. She always pitied Sarah because she didn't stand up for herself in her relationship with David; she thought, as I did, that Sarah deserved far more than the pitifully small amount of time and attention he was able to allow her; she thought, as I did, that she should have argued and ranted and wept when he wrote that letter, so calmly breaking it off with her. Alice believes a woman has a duty to fight for what she wants. She admired me for getting rid of Ralph for doing nothing much worse than criticising me and moaning about everything, she loved the way I dispatched my living-in lover, Philip Newman, when I found him in bed with her; I remember how she and I hugged each other after I'd got rid of him, she asking my forgiveness, I think, for wanting to have sex with him, and me asking her forgiveness for not allowing it.

If she knew what a craven idiot I am about Bernard, she'd really despise me. Oh yes, I acted tough, going to see that solicitor and filing for divorce as soon as he'd ignored my final ultimatum, but what good did it do me? I've never been able to forget him, he's always at the back of my mind whatever I do. Being in love makes you so bloody vulnerable. I tried all the prescribed cures – drinking too much, sleeping around, throwing darts at his photograph, even going to pottery classes – but nothing worked. He left such memories. He was so beautiful, his short, compact body, the grace of his movements, his searching eyes; conqueror, lover, betrayer. Certainly a deceiver, but honey-tongued, and unbelievably devoted to his children. And whenever I expressed surprise at the amount of attention he was

174

prepared to give them, 'I love them,' he'd say, so simply. 'And I love you, too.' Perhaps he did. In his way.

The little third-floor flat we had when we were first married, small as a nest and surrounded by trees, and I so hugely pregnant, Flora, lying on an old velvety oriental rug his parents had given us for our wedding, while he read poetry to me and the sun cast shadows of leaves on my naked belly. All that summer I felt I was living in a golden light. Drunk on warmth and the heavy gold air, I hardly went out. Bernard called at the delicatessen on his way home from work and we had delicious snacks instead of meals.

On that hot July night, I didn't realise for hours that I was in labour; I'd had two portions of a very rich Polish pudding and thought I was suffering from greed and indigestion. In any case, it was a month early and my mother had assured me that first babies were always late. By the time certain messy things had happened and we knew what it was, we decided it was too late to go to hospital. A very calm young midwife appeared eventually, who didn't turn a hair as I squeezed her, dug my nails into her, rocked on the bed, strode about singing *Cwm Rhondda*, squealed, grunted, groaned, shouted, swore and finally gave birth with all the tears and joy proper to the occasion, and probably more.

He was a beautiful baby, Gareth, dark as a little miner, and quite unperturbed by the trauma of being born – and having me as a mother. He slept in a crib in our room, and when he cried in the night, shaking his little fists about, it was usually Bernard who'd get up to fetch him. 'I'm too tired to feed him,' I'd moan, so for a while he'd nurse him, patting his back and giving him the tip of his thumb to suck. For a few moments, this would be enough to soothe the baby, and by the time he realised it wasn't quite what he wanted, I'd roused myself enough to take him. 'Lucky little devil,' Bernard would say as I put him to my breast.

I never understood why seeing him holding the baby to his chest, that quiet tenderness, always managed to rouse me sexually, far more than watching him get undressed, for instance. I used to plan in the greatest detail how I'd set about seducing him as soon as the baby was fed and changed and back in his crib, but by that time I was so tired again that all I could do was roll over to the warmth of his body and fall asleep. But I held the desire to me and in the morning my eyes were dark with love and longing. 'God help me,' Bernard would say.

I'd had to arrange to have Tom in hospital; Bernard was going to be working on some wildlife film in the south of France, my mother and my Auntie Eva coming up to look after Gareth.

Luckily Tom came early as well.

He came early because we went out one evening to an extremely erotic French film, ran all the way home from the underground station afterwards, anxious not to forget any details of a particularly athletic coupling we'd witnessed, and then tried it out instead of having the prescribed milky drink and early night.

I had to go on my own in the ambulance because it was well after midnight, the baby-sitter had long left, and there was no-one we could call on to stay with Gareth. But it was a very easy birth, the recent exercise having obviously proved beneficial, and when Bernard phoned at seven the next morning, he was told that his son was born and doing well and that he could visit whenever he wanted to. So he and Gareth were there by seven-thirty, Gareth dressed in pyjamas and dressing-gown and red boots. I was still by myself in a side ward, the baby at my side. Bernard took off Gareth's boots, popped him into bed with me and scooped Tom up from his little white cot, taking him over to the window to inspect him.

When the sister came back she scolded him for handling the baby who was premature and only five pounds in weight, but he only put his arm round her and kissed her. Then he let Gareth kiss Tom and he kissed me and then we sang Jake the Peg, which was Gareth's favourite song at that time and then shared a Mars Bar because none of us had had any breakfast.

I often think of that morning at the hospital; of the way Bernard held Tom up to the window, so full of pride and love.

I seem to remember so much love. But jealousy as well. And rage. Rage, rage, rage.

And now I'm thinking of the night's hideous dreams again, and Alice still missing. And Peter Venables, damn him, and the way he came towards me and held me down and raped me. Oh, I'm tempted to wake Sarah, but I heard her phoning the Police Station sometime before it was light, so I don't feel I can disturb her again.

Chapter 20

It's three a.m. The worst time. The lowest ebb.

I'm ill with worry about Alice and can't think about anything else. Where can she be? If she were safe she'd have rung me by this time. What's happened to her? Is she lying dead somewhere? Why haven't the police been able to find her?

'Wake me if you can't sleep,' Dilys said last night when she left my room, but how can I wake her at this bleakest hour? In any case, how could she comfort me?

I'll lie here and try to think about Alice when she was small, her little round knees and elbows. About when she was a bridesmaid that time. How old was she? About four, I think. I was so overwhelmingly proud of her, couldn't believe she was mine, that charming, exotic little creature, so full of life, so self-assured, so beautiful.

'Do you really think she's safe?' I asked Jack when we were in the pub last night.

'Of course she is. She's a force to be reckoned with, that one. Who'd get the better of her? Not Peter, that's for sure.'

He managed to comfort me for a while.

But last night seems so long ago.

We had to wait about half an hour at the side of the road before the lorry from the garage arrived to haul Jack's car out of the ditch. That took very little time, but the chap in charge insisted that it needed to be inspected back at the garage before we drove it again. And when we arrived there, there was a long hold-up; there'd been a serious accident involving three cars – four people injured, one critically – so all the mechanics were too busy to attend to us. 'Bank Holiday,' we were told over and over again.

As we sat in the cold, badly-lit office with nothing to take our attention but posters of large topless girls, I felt sure, somehow, that all the waiting would prove worthwhile, that we'd be rewarded, when we finally arrived home, with some positive news of Alice's safety. To get back to find there'd not been a single phone call was particularly daunting.

'Tomorrow,' Jack said before he left, taking both my hands in his and pressing them hard. 'We'll hear something tomorrow.' I know I should have thanked him for being such a help and support, but found I couldn't respond in any way. I hope he understood.

I ring the Police Station at half past five, but they have nothing to report. 'Don't worry,' the desk sergeant says, 'I'm sure we'll get some news very soon.'

But what news? And what if there isn't any news all day? What if the phone simply doesn't ring all day? If David rings again, I'll certainly let him know about Alice; I can't think why I didn't tell him yesterday, he'd have been very sympathetic.

For once, it seems almost soothing to think about David. So old a pain.

Jack seems to think that I chose to consider myself in love with David because he was safely married and I was afraid of a fuller commitment. I don't know. But he was what I wanted, I do know that. I loved him for twelve years and the trouble is, I can't seem to break the habit.

He might not seem a person to inspire such devotion. He's not handsome in any accepted way. He's small and dark and quiet. At school he's always very serious; he never makes jokes, rarely smiles. Not being a natural disciplinarian, he seems unable to let up in any way. He earns respect by his seriousness, his hard work, the time and effort he's prepared to give every problem as

180

it occurs, his determination to be reasonable and fair. He doesn't follow every new trend in education; our school is not noticeably different from what it was when I joined the staff thirteen years ago, but the small changes that have been made, have been carefully considered and widely discussed, and are for the better.

God, I make him sound so boring. Perhaps he is boring. He never shouts or raves at anyone, never creates dramas out of small difficulties. He's just a quiet, decent, fair-minded schoolmaster. He may not be madly popular with staff or pupils, but few, I think, dislike him.

And I love him.

Dilys can mock our sober Wednesday evenings as much as she likes; they were the best part of my life. When I loved him with my body as well as my reasoning mind. When, after making love, I lay against his skinny back, his shoulder-blades, the warm hairs on his buttocks and thighs and knew that I was happy.

Occasionally he'd arrive unexpectedly on other evenings, sometimes late at night. I never quite knew why, didn't like to probe, simply accepted his presence as a lovely bonus. Sometimes he wouldn't stay more than a few minutes; on one occasion we only had time to kiss and smile at one another before he left again. At other times he was able to stay for an hour or so. Once it was about half past eleven when he arrived and I was already in my shapeless old camel-hair dressing-gown, all my make-up cleaned off, ready to turn the lights off and go to bed.

He seemed so tense and tired that I forgot my appearance. I got him a drink and we sat together, hardly speaking, until it was well past midnight. Sometimes he seemed to need me as much as I needed him.

During the summer holidays, his sister-in-law, who lived in Montreal, would come to stay for a fortnight, and while she was there to look after his wife and keep her company, he used to have a four- or five-day break in Scotland or the Lake District, and I used to join him there.

He was a different person when he was away: light-hearted, almost light-headed at times. He was supposed to be on a

181

walking holiday, but we did very little walking. I had my car – his was left for his sister-in-law – and we used to drive about fifteen or twenty miles, a day's walk, from one hotel to another. We spent the rest of the time sitting on the hills, or in the car in bad weather. We didn't stay at any smart places, had no expensive meals. Nothing but quiet companionship during the days and long nights of happiness. I suppose that sounds boring, too.

Once, we slept on a feather bed.

It was in a loch-side village not far from Glasgow. The only hotel was full, so we had bed-and-breakfast in a small whitewashed cottage where we were the only visitors.

The little guest bedroom had sloping walls, rose-patterned wallpaper, a white painted chest of drawers and a very high double-bed.

'Will it be all right for you?' the elderly landlady asked us. 'The bed's comfortable enough, but I'm afraid it's very old. A feather bed is very old-fashioned.'

'It's lovely,' I said. 'Just what we like.'

'I don't think it will suit you. I'm sure you've got one of these beautiful modern divan beds at home.'

We looked at each other but didn't answer.

'I knew it,' she said sadly.

When we came in that evening after a meal at a pub, she was waiting for us; cocoa and biscuits laid out ready. Later, she joined us for a chat.

There we were, sitting side by side in her little front parlour as she talked about Glasgow and Edinburgh, about the price of fish, how much traffic there was on the roads, how the Royal Family were simple Scottish people at heart.

And we listened and nodded agreement with everything she said, and thought about the rose-patterned bedroom and the high old-fashioned bed.

We had oatcakes and home-made raspberry jam for breakfast. The old woman was upset because she'd run out of bacon; she didn't often have visitors, she said, not nowadays.

'This is just what we like,' we said.

'They like my old-fashioned bed and they like my oatcakes and jam for breakfast. The English are a very strange people.'

When we left, she threw her arms round me and kissed me. It was a shock. As far as I could remember, no-one had ever done such a thing before. 'Make the most of your time together,' she said. 'My husband has been dead for nearly thirty years.'

I wanted to tell her that we only had two more nights together and a very uncertain future, but I didn't. I didn't think it would have made her any happier. I just thanked her again and left.

I always knew David would have a very difficult time immediately after his wife's death; I knew he'd loved her deeply and that he'd be feeling miserable and very guilty.

But I never dreamed that he'd simply cut me off, cut me out of his life completely. Even when he has to talk to me about school matters, he can't bear to look directly at me, never smiles.

Nothing left. Nothing.

But he phoned me yesterday. Why did he want to see me again? It's almost a year, now, since Laura's death. Laura. Laura. It's not often I can bear to say her name.

'David phoned her earlier on,' Dilys said, last night. 'Wanted to see her. No wonder she's in a state.'

'I'm in a state because my daughter's missing and may be in danger. I've hardly given David a thought.'

'Good,' Jack had said. 'Don't see him again. You're getting over him.'

What nonsense. What arrogant nonsense. I'm getting used to the pain, that's all. Jack is such a fool ... All the same, he did seem concerned about me.

And he certainly seemed very worried about Alice. After he'd finally left, we thought he'd be glad to forget us, but he rang at ten and again at eleven, though Dilys had promised to let him know if there was any news.

I must have drifted off to sleep. It's now a quarter to nine and the telephone is ringing.

I almost trip over my nightdress in my hurry to get to it.

It's Gareth, Dilys's eldest son. 'Hi,' he says. 'Do you know where Mum is? I've been trying to get hold of her for days.'

'She's staying with me. Why are you phoning so early?'

''Cause I'm worried about her. I rang her three times last night. Is she OK?'

I suddenly realise that I've managed to push Dilys's ordeal right out of my mind, and feel horribly guilty. 'I'll fetch her. She can tell you herself.'

'Hey, what's wrong?'

I rush upstairs to call Dilys. She's heard the phone and is sitting up in bed.

'It's Gareth. He wants to know how you are. I didn't feel I could tell him anything.'

She jumps out of bed and I follow her downstairs and stand by the door listening. She mimes that she wants a cup of tea, but I ignore her.

'Darling, how are you?' she asks. 'How's the play getting along? When does it open? Oh, don't worry about that, that'll sort itself out before Friday. Oh, good. Have you got anyone lined up to come to see it? Oh, good. Why were you worried about me, darling? Well, do I have to be in every night of the week? As a matter of fact, Sarah's a bit under the weather and she wanted me here to keep her company. Yes of course I will. No, she wasn't a bit cross. So, when will you be home? That will be super. Yes, Hywel's fine. Yes, with Ralph and Liz. Goodbye then, darling, and good luck for Friday. I'll be keeping them crossed.'

She puts the phone down very carefully and smiles at me.

'I thought you believed in being absolutely honest with your children,' I say sternly.

'He didn't ask whether I'd been raped,' she says.

She's so brave I feel I have to make an effort as well. I make some remarks about the weather – sunny – and offer her breakfast in bed.

The Times is full of yesterday's storm. It was apparently the

184

tail end of Hurricane Archie. From America. All the Bank Holiday sport was rained or blown off.

I shouldn't think Hywel would have minded too much if they'd failed to go to the Safari Park; I think Liz likes those places more than he does. She's something high in the Girl Guides. He says she expects him to watch children's television, that she brings him teenage books from the library, when in fact he's progressed from *Five on Adventure Island* to sex and violence in one bound.

Gareth and Tom, both so brainy and highly-strung, admire Hywel enormously. Naturally they adored him when he was a toddler, starting to haul himself about after them and showing such a delightful propensity for picking up and bandying about expressions like 'legalise pot' and 'screw you', but now they take him very seriously, going to see him play rugby and even turning out with a stop-watch when he's running on the Common. They admire his blunt insensitivity and his determination to win through at all costs, though, of course, they detested the same qualities in Ralph.

'I think Gareth is your favourite,' I tell Dilys as I carry in the breakfast tray. (Gareth, after all, is the one who takes after Bernard, even in appearance.)

'Is he? I'm never sure. Gareth's the one who's fond of his mum, but Tom makes me laugh and Hywel is very big and handsome.'

'You're lucky to have three sons.'

'Yes.'

I flop down on to the bed. 'Would you believe that we could go so long without hearing a bloody word about Alice? She's been gone from this house for over thirty hours, and the police know that she's with a rapist.'

'She's probably got him cornered somewhere. We've just got to be patient.'

'I rang the Police Station at five o'clock this morning.'

'I know, love. I heard you. I was awake as well.'

Chapter 21

When I wake up it's nine-fifteen and a glorious sunny morning. There's a tray by my bed which must have been there since last night, the tea's stone-cold and the bread and butter curling at the edges.

I examine my foot, it's purple and shiny as an aubergine, but not as swollen as it was. I get out of bed, putting just a little weight on it. It's still bloody painful, but not as bad as last night.

I've got no clothes to put on. I'd like a new dress, something diaphanous and feminine. In the past I've always aimed at sensational, outrageous, feisty. Now I'd like something simple in buttercup-yellow or virginal-white.

Perhaps it's a new self I'm really after, but what can I do about that? Was I ever young and innocent? I don't think so. My mother says I used to terrify other children even when I was a toddler. At a clinic, once, she heard a mother comforting her little boy, 'It's all right, Jeremy, she can't get out of her pushchair.' I was making faces at him.

I raise the tiny sash window and lean out. There's a rich, slightly acrid country smell; ripe nettles, bracken and wet earth. There's nothing much to see except a fringe of stunted trees, mostly hazel and alder. I long to be out in the lovely green sunshine.

This morning I simply can't believe that Peter will try to keep me here against my will. I could feel him weakening last night.

If I hadn't fallen asleep when I did, I'd probably have managed to make him see sense. He's really quite a nice guy.

Is he?

Is he? If he is, what the hell happened to him? To make him attack Dilys? He *raped Dilys*. Why? How could he have done such a thing? I find myself thinking deeply about it for the first time. It suddenly seems totally incredible and unbearably sad. Did he think that making some sort of pass at her was somehow expected of him; that that was how fast, sophisticated people behaved? (He's always considered Dilys, and even my poor mother, fast and sophisticated.) I want to cry, there seems a knot in my chest so that I can't breathe.

I've probably slept too deeply and too long.

I suddenly remember a dream I had during the night. In fact it was hardly a dream, hardly more than a scene from a dream, but I suddenly recall it very vividly.

I was in some long, pleasant room, a gallery or a library perhaps, and Peter came in and stood by the door looking at me.

That's all, really. But in the dream, I remember being surprised and pleased at his appearance. He looked as he did when I first knew him; sensitive and interesting, his eyes friendly. He'd completely lost that awful caged look – wooden and hard-set – that's so unattractive.

That's all really. That's all I remember of the dream. Nothing happened. He looked as though he was happy again, that's all. Free. Free of me, perhaps.

The strange and sad thing is that this tiny fragment of a dream has made me remember how I used to feel about him. I'd almost forgotten that I was once in love with him. And that I made him fall in love with me.

I became interested in him because he was different, because he had a steady job and took himself seriously, and I lost interest in him for exactly the same reasons. And because I changed, so did he – becoming small-minded and insecure.

I'm certainly not going to blame myself for the fact that he raped Dilys, but I can't feel free of it either; not entirely.

I sink back on to the bed and cry. And for once I'm not crying out of rage or frustration, but because I feel contempt and despair for my part in it all. I can't think of anything but of how lively and self-confident he looked in my dream, and how stupid and pitiful and unmanned – or unpersoned – he looks now.

I cry until I'm really worn out; my lungs feeling painful and crushed as though I'm under a rock. (I'm under a rock, all right.)

So what's to be done? What can I do now? I dry my face on the duvet and make myself breathe deeply for a minute or two. There are some sort of brownish birds twittering rather happily outside the window. I make myself listen to them while I slowly breathe in and out. Perhaps I should simply stay here, waiting for Peter's next move. No, I must try to help him. But even if I were to take his hands and beg him to be brave and give himself up, he'd only think I was considering myself. And I couldn't blame him. When have I ever considered anyone else?

It's gone ten-thirty before I feel composed enough to hobble and hop downstairs.

Peter is sitting upright in the armchair, a blanket over his knees.

'You could have had a share of the bed,' I tell him. 'We're not exactly strangers. Did you manage to sleep?'

'I suppose I did, some of the time. Did you?'

'Yes. I had a good night.'

I make my way to the kitchen.

He follows me. 'Your clothes should be dry now,' he says. (He always hates to see me walking about naked.) 'I washed them and put them out. They've been on the line since six.'

He's wearing a pair of blue and white striped boxer shorts which I bought him last Christmas. I can't remember what he bought me, but I bet it was something very functional and practical . . . You see, I'm getting at him again.

Only my bra and pants are dry. I put them on and he passes me his now dry white shirt to wear over them.

'I'll make us some breakfast,' he says.

I sit down and watch him cutting bread and beating eggs.

He's got lovely skin, light-brown and moist-looking, and his stomach is so flat, it's almost concave.

'I haven't shaved for two days,' he says as he notices me looking at him.

He brings our breakfast to the table; a pot of tea, milk, two plump omelettes nicely speckled with brown, four pieces of bread and butter, even salt and pepper.

'Why did you fall in love with me?' I ask, my voice sounding harsher than I'd intended. 'What a bloody idiot!'

He doesn't answer. I don't think I really expect him to.

'I suppose I didn't give you much chance of getting away. I suppose it was my fault.'

'It doesn't matter,' he says. 'It's all behind us now. Eat something or you'll be ill.'

He always worried about my health. Used to buy me vitamin tablets and books about lentils.

I can remember most vividly how I used to feel about him. Before he started to lecture me and moan.

I lean forward to touch the designer stubble on his chin, but he draws away from me. For a while we sit in silence.

'I'm sorry you were so upset about the abortion, Peter. But you know, it wasn't even your baby. Honestly.'

He springs to life. His eyes blaze. 'I don't believe you. You can't be trusted. First of all, you say you didn't have an abortion. Now you say it wasn't my baby. It was. Oh, I know it was.'

'No, love, it wasn't. Why should I lie to you? At this stage? It was someone else's. You were always very careful, but this other person wasn't. His wife was on the pill and he thought I was. It wasn't your baby, Peter.'

We both try to eat. It's the first meal I've had since the day before yesterday, but I don't seem to be hungry. I'm trying to make myself eat only because he's taken the trouble to cook.

'I would still have wanted you to have it,' he says, very quietly.

190

'But I didn't want to have it. Listen, Peter, I simply didn't feel ready to be a mother. I haven't got what it takes, perhaps I never will. Anyway, I don't want to settle down. Not for years and years. I'm much too selfish. To be a mother you've got to be a sort of saint.'

We abandon all attempts at eating and sit looking at each other. I think of his cock lying limply there in his blue and white striped pants, but not of that only.

'I'm sorry I brought you here, Alice, sorry I kept you here against your will. I suppose I just wanted time to think, that's all. I wanted to kill myself – you know that – to escape from this nightmare, but you stopped me. And suddenly I seemed to get the chance to try to pull myself together. So that I can face the hell I've got to face.'

It seems unbearably sad. 'And you have pulled yourself together, haven't you? You're different today. You even look different.'

It's true. He looks as he used to – as he looked in my dream – all the heavy sullenness gone from his face. With a pang, that honestly hurts like an arrow to the heart, I realise it's because he's suddenly free of me. While I was sleeping – and I slept for over twelve hours – he must have been awake and doing some hard thinking. And the sad and awful truth is that because he seems over his obsession, I could love him again. I think I could.

'I spent most of the night in the garden. Just sitting on the seat in the garden.'

I try to put my hand on his shoulder, but he pulls away from me. I feel a bitter sort of pleasure at being rejected. At least he's sane again. It proves that much.

'I wasn't praying, I don't think so, but something cleared in my mind. I still don't accept that I raped Dilys, but I'm not absolutely sure. I do know I was desperate and desperately angry. And I know I seemed to get some pleasure from it; feeling that violence was the only thing left to me.'

He goes to the garden to fetch our clothes. 'Peter, what have I done to you?' keeps going round and round in my head. 'Oh

God, what a bloody mess.' He comes in and in a total and terrible silence, we get dressed.

Then, looking very unlike his usual self; in crumpled jacket, unironed trousers and shirt, and with a two-day growth of beard, he says he's going to the farm for another pint of milk.

When he leaves, I'm in a daze of misery, unable to think of anything but the extraordinary thing that's happened to me in this cottage. When I came here I was one person, now I seem to be another. I can't say I'm all that happy about it either. I've worked hard at being ruthless and single-minded – it isn't as easy as people imagine – and now I've become weak and sentimental. I only hope I'm not going to become one of these *caring* people, all grey and twittery.

Oh God, what can have happened to Peter? I suddenly realise he's been gone over an hour. Where is he and what can he be doing? I'm suddenly terrified that he may have killed himself after all; my throat is dry and I can feel my heart pounding. I can't bear the thought that he may be lying dead or half-dead somewhere. 'Oh Peter, what have you done?' I'm moaning, as I pull on my T-shirt and my boots. 'Whatever have you done? Whatever have I done?'

Perhaps he's waiting for me to come to look for him.

The door is still locked, but now it's no problem. My foot is nowhere near as painful as it was, so I can break a window and climb out.

I'm at the window, seeing if I can open it, when I see a woman coming up the lane towards the cottage; a youngish woman, in her early thirties perhaps, with short fair hair, wide hips and a blunt, worried face.

She raps at the door.

I try to signal that I'm locked in. I don't think she understands me, but all the same she takes a key from the pocket of her khaki jeans and lets herself in.

'I'm Rachel Webster from the farm,' she says. 'Are you all right?'

I know she's bringing me some bad news. I can feel my body stiffen, as though it's expecting a physical blow.

'I've sprained my foot, that's all. Have you seen . . . Peter?'

'Yes. He came to the house about half an hour ago and phoned the police. They've just been to fetch him.'

The room tilts once or twice and then steadies again.

'Oh thank God. I was afraid he might have . . . that he could be . . .'

I have to sit down. 'Thank God,' I say again.

'He was such a nice, good-looking young man. I can't believe he did what he says he did. My husband and I have never been so surprised. He said you were newly-weds and that your car had broken down back there in the lane. He was so polite, so nicely spoken, so concerned about you. And he told the police that he had broken bail and something about a rape charge. I thought it was some sort of a joke. I said to my husband, it's some sort of a practical joke, he's playing some sort of a practical joke on the police. But they came and took him away. I still can't believe it . . . And he said you weren't married either. What were you doing here with him? Are you his girlfriend, or did he kidnap you, or what?'

She has tears in her eyes. She's got rather a plain, square-jawed face, but her eyes are green as gooseberries and brimming over with tears.

'You weren't wrong about him. Tell your husband, you weren't wrong about him. He had a bad time, some sort of break-down, some sort of brain-storm, I think. But you weren't wrong about him. Not really.'

We look at each other, both of us swallowing hard.

'He asked us to phone your mother. He wrote down her telephone number, but when the police arrived, we found he'd taken the piece of paper with him. That's why I came. To get her number from you. Would you like to come back with me now? Can you walk? It's only about a quarter of a mile up the lane, perhaps a little less.'

'How long will it take her to come here? My mother?'

'From Shipsley? Only twenty minutes. The farm's on the main road.'

'I'll stay here then, if you don't mind. I think it would take me ages to walk a quarter of a mile.'

I give her Mum's telephone number and thank her.

'He was such a nice young man,' she says again, 'and so worried about you. You don't often see anyone as good-looking except on the telly. My husband was teasing me about him last night. Saying I'd fallen for him. That he'd better watch out.'

She tucks her shirt firmly into the waist of her jeans, pushes her hair back from her eyes. 'It's really upset me,' she says. 'We have ever so many people coming and going, but he seemed . . . Oh well, I don't know . . . different, somehow. Anyway, I'd better be off.'

She stiffens her shoulders and turns to go.

I'm standing at the door watching her leave, when a police car drives up and a young, tough-looking sergeant gets out.

'You all right?' he asks.

What should be wrong with me? 'Perfectly. Except for my foot. I sprained my foot yesterday. I'm fine except for that.'

The woman has come back and is now standing a few yards away; curious perhaps, or perhaps feeling protective towards me.

'He gave himself up,' the sergeant says. 'Venables. I've been sent to fetch you.'

He looks at us both, first one and then the other. 'He wasn't violent, at all?'

'Violent? Good Lord, no.'

'OK. I'll take you home. Have you got everything you want?'

'Do you want to go with him?' the woman asks me. 'I could still phone your mother if you'd prefer.'

'No, I 'll go now. It was my mother's car I was driving when we ran out of petrol back there in the lane. She might have difficulty getting someone to come for me. It might take her some time, anyway. I think I'll go now. It'll be quicker.'

She leaves again, giving me another long, searching look before she goes.

I get my jacket, put it over my shoulder and let the sergeant help me to the car.

'How is he?' I ask. 'Is he OK?'

'Haven't seen him. It was someone else picked him up.'

'When can I see him?'

'You'll have to ring the Station to find out. Sure you're OK?'

'Quite sure, thanks.'

'Quite sure he wasn't violent?'

'Quite sure.'

He looks obliquely at me. 'How come you tore your jacket?' he asks.

'I was sheltering under a tree during that storm yesterday and it caught on a branch.'

He studies it thoughtfully.

'It was a cheapo,' I say. 'One of these foreign ones.'

Chapter 22

As soon as the car draws up, my mother is at the window; she must have had a dreadful couple of days worrying about me. When she realises it's me, she actually puts her hand to her heart, looking as though she's about to launch into an operatic aria. I smile and wave at her.

She's at the door before I reach it. Dilys too. And what do you know, Jack Wells again.

'Thank God,' Mum says, clutching me.

We hug like anything. This woman's known me since I was a little kid and she still loves me. It's rather wonderful.

'Are you all right?' Dilys asks. 'What the hell's wrong with your foot? Why are you limping? For God's sake, tell us what happened.'

'Let me feed her first,' my mother says. 'Don't make her talk. She looks done-in. Let me get her some tea.'

'Tea? I haven't had lunch yet.'

'She's OK,' Jack says, winking at me. 'Good. I'll be off. I've got my two to pick up. Kids,' he says. 'Nothing but trouble.'

Dilys runs a bath for me while Mum's getting us a meal. When she asks whether I'd like a drink, I ask her for a cup of tea. Shows I'm getting old, I suppose.

I'm still sitting by the side of the bath when she gets back with the tea, the water only a few inches from the top.

'Come on,' she says, turning the taps off, 'what's the matter with you? Have I got to help you get undressed?'

'Yes, please. Oh Dilys, I'm in a bit of a state.'

'Of course you are. That's natural. Only, don't start to cry. That will only make you feel weaker.'

'I can't help it. I've been crying inside all day.'

'So have I. So has your mum.'

I get into a very full, blissfully warm bath smelling of sandalwood.

'How do *you* feel now?' I ask Dilys.

She doesn't answer for a moment or two. I look expectantly at her, waiting for the reassurance that's she's all right. She has to be all right.

'Not much better, love, to tell you the truth,' she says. 'I feel . . . diminished somehow. No, I'm not being melodramatic. I simply don't think I'll ever be the same person again, that's all. I don't think I'll ever be able to trust anyone again, that's all. Not in the same way. Everything's altered.'

I can't bear it. 'Dilys, shut up. Don't say that. It's not like you. How can you say that? Christ, plenty of people have terrible experiences at some time or another. Some just shrivel up, I know, but you're not one of those people. Shut up.'

My voice sounds high and very childish.

'Hey, don't get so worked up. Never mind about me. You're the one that counts at the moment.'

'Why? Don't be so humble and bloody defeatist. I can't bear it. You're more important than anyone. Don't you think I know *anything?* Don't you think I know what you've been to Mum? All this last year? Don't you think I remember how you were over that Philip Newman episode? How bloody wonderful you were to me? Christ, if you start talking about feeling diminished about something which wasn't even your fault, what hope is there for the rest of us? No, I'm serious. I'm being absolutely straight with you. If you can't pull yourself together over this, I'm finished with you. I mean it.'

Dilys blows her nose. Her eyes are puffy. She looks pretty terrible. I can't bear it.

'You've no idea what it was like,' she says. 'You've no idea how humiliated I felt, how sordid it all was.'

'Of course I have. Do you think I've got no imagination? Christ, I don't mind you being angry, even vindictive and vengeful, but as for all that rubbish about feeling diminished and never trusting anyone again, that's just not on. It's just not you, that's all.'

Now we're both sniffing.

I splash about a bit in case Mum comes up to see what all the shouting is about.

'Let's just shut up about me, OK?' Dilys says. 'You had two days with him. What was it like? Was he violent? Were you frightened?'

'No, he was just pathetic most of the time . . . well, all the time, really. Whatever happens to him, it'll be largely my fault, I'm sure of that . . . what do you think they're doing to him now?'

Dilys's voice is suddenly harsh. 'Don't worry. They won't be hard on him. They don't mind rape, and hitting your mother on the head is a bit of a joke. Don't worry about him.'

'How can I help it?'

Tears splash down my breasts and into the bath.

'At least you stopped him killing himself,' Dilys says.

'How did you know about that?'

'What else would have made you rush out to meet him at three in the morning? He was obviously threatening to kill himself. We worked that much out. You stopped him killing himself.'

'What a bloody mess, though,' I say. 'What a God-awful, bloody mess.'

'Do you know what I think you should do tomorrow?' Dilys asks.

'What?'

'Go back to Rome and take your mum with you.'

'Oh, Dilys.'

'Never mind, oh Dilys. That's what you should do. You've had a rough time. You both have. You've had two days alone

with a maniac, and she, as well as all the worry about you, had –
you'll hardly believe this – a phone call from David Noel-Smith.
Yes. He wanted to come to see her. And this when we'd only
just discovered you were missing. And she was so taken aback
that she just said she was busy and couldn't see him.'

'Oh God.'

'Yes. And of course, ever since, she's been walking about in
a daze. Wondering about his state of mind, hoping for some sort
of reconciliation with him, some sort of miracle. All that, as well
as being on tenterhooks about you.'

'Has she *told* you that she's hoping for some sort of reconciliation with him? I thought she'd—'

'Of course she hasn't. Not in so many words. We don't talk
to each other in words, we don't have to. We know each other
too well. She can talk about . . . oh, anything . . . stocks and
shares . . . anything, but I still know what's on her mind.'

'So she's expecting him to ring again? At any moment?' I
sigh, almost groan.

'She was yesterday. Today, she's a little calmer.'

'But how dare he ring her again? After the way he's treated
her? How can she allow herself to hope again? After he hurt her
so much? Can you understand it, Dilys? Christ knows, I can't.'

'Well, I suppose I can. There's nothing much worse in the
world than when someone you love stops loving you . . . Well, I
suppose famine is worse, and fire.'

'And death.'

'Losing a child is worse. The really hideous tragedies must be
worse, I suppose. But they don't happen much in this part of the
world, thank God. But the other things are certainly enough to
stir you about.'

'I certainly feel stirred about. Rattled about.'

'That's why I suggested Rome. For both of you.'

'Rome seems like a dream. It seems like something I dreamed
when I was somebody else.'

'You're tired and drained, that's all. God, I know you've had
a rotten couple of days. But when you're dressed in your mum's

new housecoat – isn't it gorgeous? – and you've got some food inside you, you'll soon be your old self again.'

'I don't want to be my old self. I prefer to stay like this.'

I feel I'm somewhere deep inside myself where I've never been before. Perhaps it's a brave new self; but I'm not too optimistic.

'I've always been afraid of feeling very deeply about anything. Afraid to be too much like Mum, I suppose, so kindled and blown about.'

'You'll never be like your mum. You're a completely different person; tougher, more outgoing, not half so nice.'

'Thanks. But I don't know. I don't think I'm tough, for a start. I feel pretty cut-up about certain things if you want to know the truth. Anyway, I'm not going back to Rome. Certainly not to Charlie's flat. What was I to Charlie but ... Well, I've had enough of Charlie. And he can stuff his job, too.'

'God, if you're going to say that you intend to devote the rest of your life to good works, I shall hit you.'

'Oh Dilys, you should have hit me lots of times before this.'

'Come on, out of that bath. You're beginning to worry me. I want you dressed and with some food inside you. Up you get.'

I get out of the bath and wrap myself in the big, warm towel she's holding out for me. (What's happening to Peter, I wonder?)

'You must be fairly well aware,' I say, 'that I'm not the noble, self-sacrificing type. I just mean that I may try to learn to paint, or something, that's all. Instead of taking the first second-rate job I'm offered. I may not mind being poor.'

'All the best people are poor,' Dilys says, 'but they don't go round recommending it. But if you've got it in you to be an artist, that's what you should be aiming at.'

'I don't know whether I've got it in me. I probably haven't. All I've done so far is to try to impress by being very outrageous and showy. If I could get rid of all the razzmatazz, I might be able to find out what's left. If anything.'

I'm suddenly more sad and dispirited than I've ever been in

my life. 'Dilys, I did have an abortion, you know. Peter wasn't lying about that.'

'Yes, love, I thought perhaps you had.'

'And it wasn't as fuckin' easy as I thought it was going to be, either. When it comes to it, it's so fuckin' sad. In fact it was fuckin' awful. Oh God, Peter so much wanted to get married and be a father. And in the end, I simply walked out on him. I simply couldn't take any more. I kept thinking about it afterwards. About him, I mean, as well as the abortion. That's why I went to Rome with Charlie. You have to take your mind off things, don't you, or you'd go mad.'

'Of course you do. Anyway, love, it was your decision, and probably the right one. What sort of life could you give a baby when you're hardly grown-up yourself? And you can't seriously think you should have let Peter blackmail you into marrying him.'

'Oh no, I wouldn't have let him do that. It wasn't even his baby. But I shouldn't have just walked out on him when he was so concerned and worried about me. He thought it was such an easy matter. That we could simply decide to settle down and be happy ever after.'

'The world is full of men who think they're the answer to all your needs.'

'If only there was something different. If only there was something altogether less demanding.'

'I was always the demanding sort,' Dilys says. 'I wanted absolutely everything. Total commitment. You don't realise your mistakes until it's too late.'

'Until it's too late. It's certainly too late now for Peter and me. Even if I wanted him, I mean. He came to his senses and wouldn't even let me kiss him goodbye.'

We sigh like two old women.

Chapter 23

What a traumatic couple of days! It doesn't seem possible that so much can happen in so little time.

The terror of discovering that Alice is missing and that Peter is almost certainly behind it.

Terror is an infrequent emotion – thank God – and it takes me back almost exactly twenty-three years to the day Geoff was drowned. There's something stubborn and untamed about Alice, too. What if a similar wild impulse – bravado? – had snatched her away from me in much the same way?

Thank God, she's safe!

When she arrives home, so childlike and bedraggled, dirty white trousers which look as though they've been slept in, some sort of biker's jacket over her shoulders, I realise that I'm in for a long bout of weeping, so I signal to Dilys, who's still here keeping me company – keeping me sane – to take her upstairs to help her get bathed and changed, while I get it out of my system without upsetting her too much.

I sit at the kitchen table, chopping vegetables and crying.

Alice is safe, but what's happened to her? Will she ever tell me? She smiled, even managed a little joke, but her eyes gave her away. Something has happened to her.

I've always counted on her being carefree and happy, bouncing back, giving at least as good as she gets. Oh Alice, don't let me down. I'm the one who's fated to be always anguished and hopeless: David's phone call, the way I completely failed to establish contact with him. I must have given him the impression of being hard and unforgiving, so why should he phone me again? Oh, why didn't I have at least the presence of mind to ask him *why* he wanted to see me? It would have been so simple. Dilys is right, he does turn me into a quivering idiot, though it's my fault rather than his.

But at least Alice is home again.

My thoughts are a hotch-potch of thankfulness and regret, happiness and sadness.

I've chopped a great mound of vegetables.

When I hear the bath being emptied, I rinse my face and try to compose myself. I can't claim that my thoughts have been subdued into any sort of order, but at least they seem to hurt less as they jostle about in my skull.

I get a meal together.

Alice thumps downstairs in my new sapphire-blue housecoat, her hair piled up on top of her head, and lies like a goddess, or a pampered odalisque, on the sofa, while Dilys and I bring in the meal; delectable sweet-and-sour pork, freshly frozen by M & S and freshly microwaved by me, and a quantity of stir-fry vegetables with ginger and soy sauce.

Alice makes enthusiastic noises, but doesn't eat much.

When I try to press more on her, she makes a despairing face.

'Mother,' I say 'give me some space,' which is a quotation from her teen years, but only Dilys smiles. 'If you'll only give me some space, I'll get it together,' she says.

After clearing away, I light some incense sticks – am I trying to create a confessional atmosphere? – and a fire, too, though it's still August.

But Dilys insists that none of us shall mention Peter until we've all had a good night's sleep, and I suppose it's a sensible idea. The poor boy has brought a great deal of trouble to us all, but even more to himself.

Neither does Alice seem keen, now, to talk about Rome. She doesn't think she'll go back there, even though I offer to pay her fare. On the whole, she thinks she can manage to live quite happily without seeing Charles Hamilton ever again.

I can't pretend to be sorry.

'You've never been in love yet,' Dilys tells her. 'It's all in front of you. The whole damned carnival.'

'I've been in love often enough,' Alice says. 'And it's always been a disaster.'

'God, I remember taking Bernard home for the first time,' Dilys says. 'My father and a convocation of uncles came to the station to meet us, all in their best dark suits. Bernard, whose parents are mild, middle-class people who breed dogs, was in a state of trance for the whole weekend as they all crowded round, interrogating him about his education, his politics, his religious beliefs, his musical tastes. I was so ashamed. I didn't think anything could ever be as bad again. But of course I was wrong.'

'Why don't you and Bernard get together? Do you ever consider it?' I want Dilys to be happy, really happy.

'God, you were pushing Ralph at me the other day.'

'He's never got married again, has he? Bernard? He was terribly upset when you divorced him. You told me that much.'

She's silent for a minute. 'He suggests it every so often,' she says then, almost in a whisper. 'But I don't think I could stand it. All his women. Perhaps when he's about seventy, he'll be ready to settle down . . . with some little bimbo.'

'Have him back. Take a chance. Throw caution to the wind.'

'No, I'm better off as I am. I'm going to start working again. No, I mean, seriously. So I'll have my career to think about. It's time I did something.'

'Why not have Bernard as well? I'm feeling generous. Ring him.'

'No. I was always so touchy and jealous with Bernard.'

'Did you talk about it?' Alice asks. 'Did he know how you felt?'

'Of course we talked about it. Sometimes we seemed to talk of nothing else. Sometimes he seemed to want to be different, but if he made promises, he always broke them. And sometimes he just shrugged his shoulders and said I had to accept him as he was.'

'You should have behaved in the same way,' Alice says. 'I mean, why not? It might have worked.'

'I thought of it often enough, but I just couldn't do it. Girls are different now. You don't believe in love as we did.'

'I believe in love,' Alice says, 'but I think I'll always be able to put myself first. I don't believe in self-sacrifice.'

'Neither did I. That's why I divorced him. When I realised he wasn't going to change.'

'But you're older now,' I say, 'more in control, more tolerant. Why don't you phone him, tell him about the rape, how devastated you've been, and ask him to come to see you?'

'No. He's bound to hear about it eventually from one or other of the boys. And he can come without being asked if he comes at all. Anything could happen, I suppose. That's what makes life bearable, I suppose.'

Anything could happen. *I'd like to see you, Sarah.* Oh, shut up, shut up. Why can't I stop thinking about it?

We sit around far too long. We're too tired to talk much, but we seem to need each other's company.

Chapter 24

And then it's the next morning, and Dilys and I, both admitting to a reasonable night, are having coffee and rolls in the kitchen, Mozart on the radio, the postman bringing nothing more alarming than a picture-postcard from St Ives.

The slanting sun lights up a corner of the pine dresser and two of my blue and white plates in a way I've never seen before. I get the feeling in my middle-aged bones that something – what? – is about to happen. The moment is like the beginning of a new play, and I cross my fingers for something light; a pleasant domestic piece with no violence or belly laughs.

There's no sign of Alice, though it's almost ten-thirty. For a few minutes we discuss whether she should see a doctor about her foot, both of us knowing that she isn't going to, whatever we think or say.

'She's been going her own way for years,' I tell Dilys. 'She's not likely to start listening to me at this stage.'

'She hasn't done too badly.'

'I suppose not. Do you know, I don't think I'm going to worry too much about her from now on. She seems pretty well in charge of her life, doesn't she?'

'I'll say she does. She's certainly managed to get us where she wants us.'

Dilys sounds rueful, but as I'm about to question her, she springs to her feet. 'I must go,' she says, frowning at her watch and shaking it. 'Hywel's due back for lunch and I've got to take him shopping this afternoon.'

'Oh don't. Not this afternoon. You're not up to it. Look, I'll take him if you like.'

'No, love. I've got to pull myself together. It may do me some good to be out and about. I've got to get him some shirts for school.'

'God. School next week. And I've got a hopeless Upper Sixth.'

'You always say that. But your results are always brilliant.'

'I may give in my notice and go to Spain.'

'And I may go to Hollywood. This could be the day when that famous director asks for me.'

After washing up and putting some clothes in the machine, I wander out to look at the garden and before I realise it, I've got my gardening gloves on and a trowel in my hand.

The earth is black and juicy after the recent heavy rains; the weeds, even the dandelions, slipping out of the ground as though oiled. The bees are like little buses in and out of the lavender. In no time, I'm planning the autumn planting and transplanting.

If ever I do leave here – for Spain or Italy? – I'd miss the garden. The house is just any house, but I've left my mark here: stone walls, borders of blue and silver, a great deal of white – I've even got a white-berried holly tree – though hardly anything that can be described as showy. Dilys, who likes dazzling displays of bedding plants, thinks it's all a bit contrived and precious, but David used to say . . . but never mind that, never mind that.

When Alice appears, I'm surprised to discover that it's almost three o'clock.

'Is this jacket worth mending?' she asks me. 'Or shall I dig a hole and bury it?'

I straighten my back, wipe my hands on my jeans and take it from her.

'You certainly can't do anything with it till it's dried out. Whatever happened to it? Where did you get it, anyway?'

'Its history is entirely sordid. Perhaps I should burn it. Or bury it.'

'Why bother to do anything so melodramatic. Just put it in the bin.'

She does.

Then she limps away to get us some bread and cheese and beer.

'By the way, I went to the Police Station earlier on,' she says when we've started eating. 'Yes, I got a taxi. Anyway, Peter didn't want to see me. Wouldn't see me.'

'Perhaps that's a good sign,' I say gently. 'Perhaps he's ... you know ... started to accept that it's all over between you. Perhaps it's a good sign.'

She doesn't reply. Her eyes tell me nothing and I haven't the courage to question and probe.

We stay in the garden for the rest of the afternoon.

August isn't quite over, but the thin, rusty smell of autumn is in the air. We haven't had much of a summer. Autumn may be better; Michaelmas days, mild and peaceful, long nights returning.

I still feel restless, my nerve endings taut with waiting. 'May I ring you again, Sarah? To suggest another meeting?' Oh, why doesn't he ring again? Why doesn't he consider my feelings? Did he ever consider my feelings? Was I ever much more to him than a comfort and balm? Did he ever love me? Perhaps I was always satisfied with too little. Perhaps Dilys was right all along.

'Listen, Mum, why don't we take Dilys to the South of France for the rest of the week?' Alice asks. 'Why not? We can take Hywel as well. In your new car. It'll do us so much good. We could all do with a holiday, couldn't we? We've all had a rough time.'

She suddenly looks herself again, vivid and expectant, ready for the next adventure.

I remember her as a baby of six months. Studying leaves, clouds, birds. Sitting up and watching. Her eager expression. As though she couldn't wait to touch and taste everything. As though she couldn't wait to be out of her pram and off. The South of France? Why not?

She becomes suddenly grave. 'Only we've got to get the bloody car back first. PC Plod said we had to fetch it last night, that it was a hazard and all that rubbish. I suppose I'll have to get Dilys to take me to fetch it.'

She shudders at some bad memory.

'Poor love. It hasn't been easy for you, has it?'

'I deserved it, Mum. Peter isn't really a thug. I drove him to it. God knows I didn't mean to, but I did.'

'Nonsense. However badly you behaved, it didn't give him the right to turn into some sort of . . . animal.'

'I know. But that's what happened. And now it's going to be hell for him, isn't it? He was so pathetic, Mum. I'm honestly not trying to defend him, I'm simply telling you that he really is suffering now.'

I suppose she's right. But does she have any idea what Dilys went through? Physically and mentally. Of course not. Only I know that. Perhaps it's just as well she doesn't know the half of it.

'I'll ring the garage and get them to fetch it,' I say. 'The police can give them directions. What's money? If we're going to the South of France, I'll end up broke anyway.'

'Hey, Mum, what's got into you? Are you all right?'

As soon as I finish phoning the garage, Alice announces that Jack Wells has just driven up.

'Why is he here again?' she asks. 'You dislike him, I thought.'

'Jack? I don't dislike Jack. Not at all.'

'He thinks you do.'

'He's a fool, then. I like him. I like him very much.'

'Well! Well, in that case I'd better let him in, hadn't I?'

Why is she looking at me so slyly?

Jack shoulders into the room; a man with something to say

210

and in a hurry to say it. He's often infuriated me in the past, but I've always admired his toughness and drive.

'How are you both?' he asks. He studies Alice's face for a moment as though looking for signs of wear and tear. Not finding any, he smiles at her.

Then he turns to me. 'I'm afraid I've got some bad news for you, Sarah. I've just been over to school to see the new time-table.'

'Hey, if you two are going to talk school, I'll go and make a pot of tea,' Alice says. She hobbles from the room, banging the door behind her.

Jack looks unusually grave. 'What is it?' I ask, gripping the arms of my chair. This is something more than timetables.

'It's Noel-Smith. He's had some sort of breakdown during the holiday and they're letting him go straight away. He's going to join some religious community in Norfolk. Some Anglican place. That's probably what he wanted to tell you when he phoned. He probably wanted you to know before anyone else.'

I'm fighting through a wave of blackness.

He used to sit in that chair where Jack is sitting now. He always looked so much younger – sometimes quite boyish – when he was here. I remember how he used to look up at me, that tender smile. How very happy I used to be ... How very foolish.

'I thought it might have been something like that,' I say quietly. 'Who's taking over?'

'Sarah, are you really all right? Or are you just being brave?'

I can't even think about that. 'Who's taking over?' I ask again.

'Brenda Johns is going to be Acting Head for a couple of months. Until someone else is appointed.'

'She'll be good.'

I'd like to see you, Sarah. May I ring up again to suggest another time? Mightn't he have guessed the direction my thoughts would have taken? Why couldn't he have said, 'Sarah, I've been taken ill and have to leave school. I wanted you to be the first to know.' Oh David, I hardly existed for you, did I? You thought your suffering gave you the right to disregard what I might be going through. You were never really concerned about me, were you?

'Of course that means that Head of Special Needs will be vacant and I intend to apply for it.'

'Good.'

I'd like to see you, Sarah. Oh stop it, stop it. Over is over. Or at least almost over. You never really loved me, David, did you?

'I thought you'd be pleased. If only to get rid of me from the English Department. After all, I'm practically illiterate.'

Relax, he's teasing. 'I think you're a very good teacher. And you'll be an excellent Head of Department. You care about people.'

You care about people. It was kind of you to come to tell me about David. It can't have been easy.

Alice comes back in with a pot of tea.

I've still got a meal to think about. I'll do something really elaborate, something which takes up all my concentration. Thank God for work, even the small routine tasks. Thank God for washing and ironing and shopping and cooking.

'Has Mum told you we're going to France tomorrow?' Alice asks Jack. 'You don't take sugar, do you?'

'No. No, she hasn't. How are you going? When are you setting off?'

I leave the conversation to them. It's as much as I can do to listen, to take tiny sips of tea, to try to appear normal, or at least fairly normal.

'I've just phoned Dilys. She can't believe it. She hasn't got any money, but I told her Mum was going to pay. You are, aren't you, Mum? Oh, and Hywel has got thirteen pounds which he's willing to chip in. As long as he doesn't have to go to any museums or talk any French.'

'Fair enough. Where will you go?'

'To Provence, I think. That's where Mum and I usually make for. For the sun and the wine. Have you had a holiday this year?'

'No, I couldn't seem to get it together. Lena took the kids pony trekking. Something she and the other woman were organising. Fourteen children all told. Stevie loved it, but old Fred said he'd rather have stayed home with me. Too many little girls, he said, and too many big horses.'

'I haven't seen them for ages. I'll come round sometime – as soon as we get back. Give them my love.'

I'm roused by the warmth in Alice's voice. What a great deal Jack went through last year. But, suffering myself, and knowing he had plenty of young friends and colleagues on the staff, I hardly spared him a moment's sympathy.

I do now, Jack.

Love, damn it, makes victims of us all. But most of us are able to rally our resources and make some different sense of our lives. I'm sure you'll manage it, Jack. And what about me? Haven't I suffered long enough?

'David has had some sort of breakdown,' I tell Alice. 'He's giving up the headship and joining a religious community. Jack came over to tell me. Thought I should be one of the first to know.'

'God almighty. Two mental breakdowns in one fuckin' week. And I don't feel too good myself.'

'She's not as callous as she pretends,' I tell Jack.

'I know.'

Of course you do. Why do I always underestimate you? All the same, please drink your tea and go. I need some time to myself. Too much has happened today, far too much. Was I mad to agree to this trip to France? Will I be able to bear it? Having to pretend to be excited and happy? Oh, David, what if you ring me again to say goodbye? To explain things? And I'm not here?

'Well, I'd better be going,' Jack says, getting to his feet. 'Thanks for the tea, Al. Have a great time in France.'

He turns to me. 'Well done,' he says. 'It's the best bloody thing you could do.'

'Is it?' I ask him. 'Is it really? I'm not at all sure.'

I stand up facing him and he's suddenly gripping my hands. 'I'm sure,' he says, 'Sometimes it's the only thing. Change. A

213

change of scene, a change of direction. The best thing.'

'I'll see you next week, then.'

'Next week.'

Change. It must be possible, it must. I've had almost a year to reconcile myself to the break from David – oh David, one day I may be able to write to you, giving you cheerful little snippets of news about school – and I'd more or less managed it. That phone call was only a small hitch in the healing process and now I'm back on course. And Alice is very nearly herself again and Dilys will be able to put her ordeal behind her because she's incredibly tough and brave. I shake my head so that not a single tear shall settle in my clear, outward-looking eyes.

Alice comes back from seeing Jack to the gate. She gets a map of France from the desk, unfolds it and brings it over to me.

Two Loves
Siân James

Rosamund Gilchrist is restless. She has lived her life so far in supporting roles: widowed third wife of the much older Anthony, a famous poet; mother of the enchanting Joss; daughter of eccentric divorced parents, and mistress of her neighbour, Thomas. But that affair is now over and Rosamund must face facts – that if she wants anything of her own she must venture out of her country sanctuary and make a life for herself.

Then Rosamund is drawn into a feud between Anthony's mistress and his second wife, still bitter after the breakdown of their marriage and determined to stop the publication of erotic poems which he wrote for his mistress years before. Compassionate, impulsive, naïve, Rosamund feels compelled to travel to London to mediate. And in the charged atmosphere of still-burning passions, she finds herself facing new experiences, and challenges, which change her life in unexpected ways ...

"A superb ear for dialogue and a marksman's eye for revealing detail"   *Sunday Times*

"Siân James writes fluently and with lively humour about the complexities of family life"   *The Times*

Fair Exchange
Lynne Reid Banks

Sometimes strangers with little in common can forge friendships as deep as their differences.

Judy's life in London is dominated by her political causes – she is determined to make a difference. While Judy organises rallies and stands in all-night demos, Harriet tends her garden, and sometimes drinks too much. She has never fought for a cause in her life.

A chance meeting will change their lives and mark the start of an unconventional friendship, a friendship that forces both women to question their beliefs – and ultimately to seek the life the other has ...

From the critically acclaimed author of *The L-shaped Room*.

"Lynne Reid Banks displays a wonderful comic touch ... We should have more of her."   *Daily Telegraph*

"Lynne Reid Banks has that rare gift of evoking a scene or situation in little more than a line"   *The Times*

"A beautifully crafted novel ... from first chapter to last it's very hard to put down."   *Birmingham Post*

The Angels of Russia
Patricia Le Roy

In the cold war Soviet Union, even passion is political ...

On a study trip to Leningrad, literature student Stéphanie meets Sergei, an enigmatic young dissident. Stéphanie had fallen in love with a fairy tale image of Russia – full of palaces and aristocrats; Sergei offers to show her just how different the reality is. Even in the supposedly enlightened days of Gorbachev, Sergei is in constant danger because of his political beliefs. So when he asks Stéphanie to agree to a marriage of convenience so that he can leave the country she is unable to refuse him.

Despite the platonic nature of their relationship, Stéphanie finds herself increasingly attracted to her mysterious new husband. But when Stéphanie introduces Sergei to her aunt Marina, a Russian who defected to Paris whilst accompanying her father on a political mission, he appears to know more about Marina's past than Stéphanie. Could Marina be the real reason why he has come to Paris? As it becomes increasingly clear that Sergei is harbouring more than one secret, Stéphanie is forced to question whether their first meeting was as accidental as it seemed

"Fascinating: full of surprises and strong characters"
The Bookseller

The very best of Piatkus fiction is now available in paperback as well as hardcover. Piatkus paperbacks, where *every* book is special.

The prices shown above were correct at the time of going to press. However, Piatkus Books reserve the right to show new retail prices on covers which may differ from those previously advertised in the text or elsewhere.

Piatkus Books will be available from your bookshop or newsagent, or can be ordered from the following address:
Piatkus Paperbacks, PO Box 11, Falmouth, TR10 9EN
Alternatively you can fax your order to this address on 01326 374 888 or e-mail us at books@barni.avel.co.uk

Payments can be made as follows: Sterling cheque, Eurocheque, postal order (payable to Piatkus Books) or by credit card, Visa/Mastercard. Do not send cash or currency. UK and B.F.P.O. customers should allow £1.00 postage and packing for the first book, 50p for the second and 30p for each additional book ordered to a maximum of £3.00 (7 books plus).

Overseas customers, including Eire, allow £2.00 for postage and packing for the first book, plus £1.00 for the second and 50p for each subsequent title ordered.

NAME (block letters)_____

ADDRESS_____

_____

I enclose my remittance for £_____

I wish to pay by Visa/Mastercard   Expiry Date:_____
